KAIROS

KAIROS

A NOVEL

Joanne Lehman

Herald Press
Scottdale, Pennsylvania
Waterloo, Ontario

Library of Congress Cataloging-in-Publication Data

Lehman, Joanne, 1950-
Kairos : a novel / Joanne Lehman.
p. cm.
ISBN 0-8361-9313-X (pbk. : alk. paper)
1. Women social workers—Fiction. 2. People with mental disabilities
—Services for—Fiction. 3. Thanksgiving Day—Fiction.
4. Mennonites—Fiction. 5. Farmers—Fiction. I. Title.
PS3612.E3545K35 2005
813'.6—dc22
2005019195

KAIROS, A NOVEL
Copyright © 2005 by Herald Press, Scottdale, Pa. 15683
    Published simultaneously in Canada by Herald Press,
    Waterloo, Ont. N2L 6H7. All rights reserved
Library of Congress Catalog Card Number: 2005019195
International Standard Book Number: 0-8361-9313-X
Printed in the United States of America
Book design by Sandra Johnson
Cover by Sans Serif
Cover illustration by Jill-Ann Cherofsky.
Credit for the excerpt from "What Is This Place" on page 26: Text and
arrangement © 1967, Gooi en Sticht, Bv., Baarn, The Netherlands. All
rights reserved. Exclusive agent for English-Language countries: OCP
Publications, 5536 NE Hassalo, Portland, OR 97213. All rights
reserved. Used with permission.
Excerpt from the Seamus Heaney poem "The Peninsula" on page 87 is
from Poems, 1965-1975 (New York: Farrar, Straus and Giroux, 1981).
Excerpt from "For the Beauty of the Earth" on page 201 is by Folliott
S. Pierpoint and appears in Hymnal: A Worship Book (Scottdale, Pa.:
Mennonite Publishing House, 1992).

12 11 10 09 08 07 06 05   10 9 8 7 6 5 4 3 2 1

To order or request information, please call
1-800-759-4447 (individuals); 1-800-245-7894 (trade).
Web site: www.heraldpress.com

*To the Beloved
who work and hope.*

Prologue

THERE ARE A FEW THINGS you need to know before I tell you about that strange, unforgettable autumn.

Even now, all these years later, sometimes when I'm driving along country roads in Ohio's Addison County I'll see cows and horses sharing an end-of-season pasture, or notice a few brittle cornstalks left standing in a field. And it all comes back in a rush.

When I think of that time, there is still a dull ache. But I also know I've made peace with *what is*. Sometimes I say to myself, "This is my *life*. This is *our* life." I suppose that isn't particularly profound, but it's enough to remind me to live *this* day. Today is *kairos* too—a moment of grace and opportunity.

Back then, I worked, as I still do, at Helping Hands. I'm a case manager for people with mental disorders. I used to call them "my People," which now sounds too possessive. It was only because I cared so much and because there weren't good words to describe our connection. It's a lot better than calling them consumers, which is the prevailing term these days. Maybe, as the social worker professional guidebook says, I'm a "resource manager."

Helping Hands has a stodgy mission statement announcing "responsive service provision; a broad array of assistance." But my mission statement is "do unto others . . . ," the Golden Rule. I link my People to services, which means, for instance, I take Harry to Goodwill to buy a sofa bed with the money held by his payee, then arrange to have it delivered to the fifth apartment he's moved into in as many years, because he lives half his life in the psychiatric hospital and keeps getting uprooted from hospital to group home to independent living.

What I especially remember noticing that year was the quality of light—late afternoons, in particular, were ethereal. I don't think the landscape was ever as beautiful before or since. But perhaps it was simply that I suddenly saw everything in greater detail because of life's unfolding.

Without realizing it, something within me moved ever so slightly, and I was no longer the capable, professional public servant who followed protocol to the letter and kept passionate hope alive in the face of impossible odds. I made a choice. Such a small decision. Later I looked back and realized that choice—to meet with Darwin at Mel Martin's farm on a weekend in October—had taken me to a place I'd never imagined.

When I try to trace events backward to the beginning of the *kairos* journey, I end up in a cabin in springtime, in Stony Ridge State Park with Reverend Rhonda, as we sometimes called her. That weekend, we met on the path.

"Join me for a walk," she urged. "I have things to show you."

As we walked, Rhonda stopped to point out things along the trail. She showed me the Allegheny mound ants and afterward we wandered toward a wall of solid rock. We climbed over logs, and Rhonda showed me the clumps of coltsfoot with sage-colored stems and the tips of fiddlehead fern pushing through.

We rested on a cool, flat rock and I started telling my story. Our conversation tapered off and started up again as if it had an internal rhythm. I've often thought that this is perhaps the most healing thing we can ever do for another, to simply listen.

As I talked, a hawk screamed. His tail glowed red in the sun as he swept the sky, tracing a great arc. Perhaps he gave me this voice, because after that I could tell Rhonda the things that needed to be said. It wasn't so much that she needed to know them, but that I needed to say them.

"Rhonda," I said, "I want to tell you about the work I do, about my mother, whose social activism brought me to become 'Angie, the Helping Hands Case Manager,' and about my father, who took me to the farms and loved the earth."

The things that happened after that talk with Rhonda—the suffering and slipping away of my soul, and how it was returned to me—that is the subject of this spiritual travelogue, my *kairos*.

1

IN OCTOBER, I preferred my colored leaves with sun. That said, I don't always get what I want.

The Saturday morning I'd planned to meet Darwin I threw on some khakis and a generic T-shirt. Over top, I pulled a claret-colored sweatshirt—a freebie from the local public radio station. In stocking feet, I stepped into the garage and pressed the automatic door opener. I grabbed my Nikes from a duffel bag in my dusty Nissan Sentra and sat on the step, tying them as I observed the cloudy sky. I thought imprecisely about my plans.

I was going to drive somewhere. Just get into my car and drive. In one part of my mind, the conscious part, I had no agenda. And yet I did. It was still too early in the day to admit I was doing something I didn't understand or approve of.

If I'd bothered to look just then, I would have seen the truth written in Darwin's directions to his uncle's farm, which were scrawled on a scrap of paper torn from a yellow legal pad and tucked into the front pocket of my department-store designer bag. I'd decided that day to skip the gym, the treadmill, and the weight circuit. I'd called Rhonda last evening and told her I wouldn't make it for racquetball.

It was recycling day, so I loaded the pile in the corner of the garage into my trunk and told myself I had plenty of time for errands on my way out of town. I fetched the newspaper from the box and threw it on the seat.

As I backed out the driveway, my blue Cape Cod

looked at me disapprovingly. Its gray eyes mocked me and its flowered mouth curved slightly. But a second glance revealed tacit permission. I was doing only what I needed to do. The time was right.

Sometime later, I cruised into Booneville and stopped for breakfast. It was the kind of town you forgot about until you drove through it again—a collection of buildings changed little since they were built fifty years earlier. The restaurant used to be a truck stop, but the trucks stopped stopping.

As I entered, the door wheezed shut on its worn pneumatic arm. The fragrance of hash browns and bacon helped me decide what I would order before I sat down. The coffee was weak and the cup a regulation heavy weight, with lots of stains and scratches.

At the largest table, a group of retired men wearing Indians shirts and Browns caps sat talking about taxes and too many levies on the ballot. A township trustee circulated with his blue and white campaign flyers and then settled in. Soon they were discussing the potholes that still hadn't been fixed, a crime when you took into account the fact we were heading into a season that would generate more. For my part, I thought the failure to pass the social services levy was more heinous. I'd have said so, given half a chance.

I opened the newspaper and pretended to read, but my mind was somewhere else. I felt as gray as the sky, as tired as the wallpaper across the room with its greasy blue teapots and green checked background. A perennial self-analyzer, I knew the reason for my malaise. In the ten years since I'd returned to Ohio to work as a case manager, the fading light of fall had become ever harder for me to live with.

My mind was on myself, not on my work that gray morning. I made an unofficial diagnosis: I was sure I had SAD—seasonal affective disorder.

The week before, I'd stopped at Nature's Medicine Shoppe to look for an herbal remedy, which was unusual for someone like me, a proponent of medication to fix moods. But SAD is a simple mood disorder, some say readily treated by sitting under a special light. But it's too expensive and I'm too busy. When would I have time to sit for that long? Herbs are worth a try. I would see what I could do on my own to push back the darkness and the ever-present threat of despondency. Understand, I wasn't like Darwin and the rest of my caseload. Only a little sad, probably lonely, tired and too busy.

The first cup of thin coffee and the scrambled eggs and bacon were enough to awaken my conscience. I should know better than to mix my personal and professional lives, but that's exactly what I was about to do. I felt a twinge of guilt when I thought of Barbara Delaney, my clinical director. But, after all, no one would ever know. That's what I tried to believe as I sat there eating breakfast, reading the newspaper, and diagnosing myself.

I pulled out the yellow paper with Darwin's directions and looked at it again. Darwin had somehow wormed his way through the social worker façade I'd worked so hard to construct. He was likeable and interesting to me in a way I couldn't explain to anyone. Then too he was making some great progress and I didn't want anything to stand in his way, least of all the stupid rules we make about interpersonal stuff with our People.

"Can I get you more coffee, ma'am?" The white-haired waitress with arthritic hands poured a second cup and took my empty plate to the kitchen, leaving me to finish contemplating how I'd ended up there.

℮

It was at Farnswalters Tree Nursery last Monday that this whole thing really had begun, I guess. I had to pick up Darwin; transportation is a huge problem for our People who try to work. We had a program called Job Readiness Training. "Never underestimate the values of a taxpayer," I thought in my more cynical moments. But the truth is, we all believed in the value of hard work. And besides, work was a place to make friends and build "self-efficacy," as I often reminded my People.

That day, Darwin looked so comfortable in his off-brand jeans, faded, plaid flannel, and mulch-stained athletic shoes. He pulled a water bottle off its belt holder, then fished a plastic pill holder out of his pocket. Not at all self-conscious, he threw the pills down the back of his throat and swallowed. I glanced at my watch and reminded myself to make a note in his chart. "Medication schedule followed in workplace. Steel-toed work boots needed."

"Ready to go?" I asked in my best case-manager voice.

"Oh, already, Angel?" Darwin flirted in his mocking tone as he looked into the branches above us. He always called me Angel instead of Angela. I suspected he knew my real name and did it on purpose. It made me nervous.

I stood there feeling unnatural, frozen, stiff. A flock of geese honked up from the pond. Darwin lit a cigarette as we watched the lead goose move into position.

Standing there in the crisp air that day must have reminded me how tired I was of noise and stupid technology and mental health. All day I'd been racing around in my car, trying to get to places on time. I'd felt out of breath and overwhelmed. And it was only Monday.

Unaccustomed anger had erupted inside me. I was suddenly furious about the increasing demands at the agency. Exhaustion was taking over. I was tired of being unreal, playing a part, filling a role, being some kind of savior, or at least a fussy mother, to so many needy people. I was fraying at the edges. The anger was a sign, I suppose, but I didn't recognize that.

Darwin seemed to suspect nothing. He exhaled cigarette smoke and stared intently at me. My skirt suddenly felt too short, my modest neckline, too low. I broke the spell. "Come on," I said. "Let's get going."

"Hey, can we stop by Drug World on our way back? I need to grab a pack of cigarettes."

In the car, Darwin swung his arm up over the seat, almost touching my shoulder with his fingers, acting cocky—like I'd picked him up for a different reason.

I pretended not to notice.

He edged closer and locked his eyes onto the dashboard just above the glove box. "Mel's taking me out to the farm end of the week—you know, my uncle Mel's farm—to help him plant garlic. Why don't you come get me *out there?*"

I shrugged. "We'll see."

He was still speaking to the glove box. "You got nice hair. I liked the way you looked back there under the tree, Angel baby." I smelled his cigarettes as his dirty hand brushed the back of my head and quickly came to rest on the seat. He leaned closer.

"You could bring me home. . . . You gotta come." His breath smelled of smoke. But his clothes still held a hint of the fresh outdoors. "Can you come an' get me on Saturday? Please, Angel. Mel has chores to do and I'm a big bother to him."

I heard the plaintive tone of one of my People, begging for someone to care, and I forgave his indiscretions. To be honest, I heard a hint of something in Darwin's tone that I needed: kindness. Something I hadn't felt from anyone for a long, long time. I sighed and considered. "We'll see."

℘

The arthritic waitress returned with my bill and laid it face down on the table. She'd signed her name on the back with "Thanks for coming!" She smiled and squeaked off in her white Hush Puppies to pour more coffee for the retired table.

I got back in my car and headed south. I'd wasted the better part of a morning eavesdropping on old men and trying to feel better about myself—something that was getting harder and harder to do.

"Darwin," I was thinking, "I hope you appreciate this. I wouldn't do this for just anyone."

Had I bothered to take even a moment or two to gather some insight, I'd have realized Darwin was taking me places I hadn't planned to go. It had started weeks earlier with the conversations of two people traveling together through life. Conversations we'd been having, which were moving us both. Used to be we'd ride from Hilldale to Middletown to see his therapist and he wouldn't say two words—just grunt in response to my questions. I'd written in my notes: *Nonresponsive and sullen. Check with Dr. Anthony about possibly increasing the antidepressant. Watch for lethargy or mood swings.* I'd been trying all this time to figure Darwin out, to help him. I cared about him so much, just like I care about all my People, and next thing I knew, he was flirting with me!

What am I doing? Where am I going? I'm driving out into nowhere—to a farm—to pick up Darwin, even though it's Saturday, my day off. Later on, I realized that the farm wasn't nearly as far away as it seemed that afternoon. It was as if I had entered a time warp of errands, a long late breakfast, a wrong turn, then driving up into Stony Ridge and following the Ohio byway till it met the Lincoln Highway. An odd and confused journey, even for someone as directionally challenged as I am.

16

My eyes wandered over the fields, which were still green, to the hardwoods, which were changing to shades of red and gold. The murky sky spoiled the small enjoyment I might have gained from the scenery. On the lonely hills here and there farm animals were still out to pasture. They stood staring vacantly at the mature cornstalks.

Three skinny dogs loped silently alongside my car for the length of a long cornfield. The field was in an odd, unsightly state of ripening, moving slowly from green to brown, but not yet brittle.

The road took an unexpected turn, and a minute later I wasn't sure I was on the right one anymore. It was still paved, but seemed narrower. I didn't see any of the landmarks Darwin had described—an old water tower, two oil wells, the Wooden Nickel beer joint, as he called it with more familiarity than I'd appreciated. Still, I drove on. Maybe I was grateful for the time alone, the quiet car, the hills and valleys I was traveling.

The long, wet summer had yielded lush foliage. Roadsides had grown thick with wild carrot and blue sailor. Timothy and alfalfa had escaped the fields and climbed into the ditches. Though township crews had mowed it down in late July, it had all sprung back and mixed into the goldenrod. Weed bouquets tumbled over fencerows, providing an understory of the colors everyone had been waiting for. Finally, they were at their peak of brilliance—or would have been if only there'd been some sunshine.

Working as a case manager for Helping Hands in Hilldale, Ohio, I didn't usually stray too far from the county seat during the week. I went where my caseload took me. Public housing and group homes are clustered, for the most part, on the back edge of town. I didn't do country roads very well. Maybe that explains how I'd managed to get myself lost only a few miles from home. Maybe I was so self-absorbed I would have lost my bearings anyway.

Hilldale was a pleasant town, with a population of about 25,000. It had managed to keep its downtown alive despite a sprawling new shopping center that covers several old farms on the east side. I liked downtown, with its coffee shop, Common Grounds, and used bookstore where the students at Hilldale College unload their literary classics for a little extra cash.

"It makes perfect sense for me to drive out here to pick up Darwin on a weekend," I reasoned as I kept driving. "And if I spend some extra time with him, off the clock, who cares? Darwin's making a lot of progress and the farm's good for him."

The tragedy of his disability was that it affected everything, even driving. When you're disabled and on strong medications, you shouldn't drive. And anyway, on public assistance, you can't afford a car. You can't afford a social life either. You're edged out because your brain doesn't have the right chemical makeup, and people notice that.

A few weeks earlier we'd finally cleaned out Darwin's old Horizon so it could be towed to the junkyard. The whole thing took a lot longer than it had to. He was quite the collector. He stopped to show me the Louis L'Amour paperback, heavily underlined and yellowed with age. Told me the whole story. He'd marked the map in the back of the book as if he'd been to the places. There were other books, an old poetry paperback, a pictorial anthology of the Vietnam War, and a spiral notebook with handwritten poems scrawled in large, uneven letters. We'd found pens and cigarettes and fake Indian relics, a cheap western string tie with a silver sliding clasp, and a large Swiss Army knife with the fork extended.

Most telling of all was an old leather wallet I pulled from under the seat. We stopped and looked through the pictures of his high-school friends. The photos were from another era, like the hand-tooled billfold stitched with rawhide, which was probably made during a stay in the state hospital. I didn't ask.

We saved the precious velvet picture of Jesus in a black frame. Jesus going up into heaven, his feet almost on fire. Darwin propped it inside his front door, where it will probably sit for years.

Somewhere I still have the poems he gave me that day. I suppose I shouldn't have taken them. But better that than the painting. Heaven knows I don't go for velvet paintings— or cheap religious art of any kind, for that matter.

For more than ten years I'd case-managed like the professional social worker I was. I tried to do everything by the book, but there were more and more rules to follow and things to document, and I was sick of it. Sometimes I just wanted to act human. Maybe that's why I'd taken the poems, why I'd taken off that morning to bring Darwin back home from his uncle's farm.

My shoulder was aching again. That happened a lot when the weather was changing. A fleeting thought about my ex came along with the soreness. I clenched the steering wheel as if to put the pain where it belonged.

I looked at the road ahead of me, wondering, "Have I missed a turn? Where is that turnoff? Now what road is that?" It was anyone's guess. I was not that far from home, but I guessed I was distracted with all the backwash of thoughts about Darwin and all. I hated getting lost.

I tightened my grip. Surely I'd recognize something soon. Sometimes getting lost in Ohio isn't so bad. It depends on the terrain. Most of the roads are laid out in a grid dividing the land into sections. In pioneer days the sections were quartered and settlers built their houses and barns at the center, making it easy to reach their fields.

This made for farms with long lanes. Sections make townships and townships make counties. Occasionally, a road will meander alongside a stream like this one did, and when you're lost, you just keep going until you find yourself.

If you want to know the truth, I kept at social work because when I saw changes in one of my People it challenged my creativity. I was edging Darwin closer to real life than he'd been in a while. I was taking a risk. I knew he might decompensate. (I hate that word, but I still use it sometimes. It's shorthand for a relapse. I guess it's accurate, because when you have a serious mental illness you have to compensate. But there's an element of fault-finding in that word, and I don't like it.) The goal is for People to be normal, whatever that is. Anyway, Darwin hadn't decompensated in more than four years.

There's nothing I would have liked more than for Darwin to be normal. And driving out there on that road that afternoon—by then it *was* afternoon—I almost convinced myself something was changing. I'd decided I was just an eternal optimist—for my People if not always for myself.

I opened the car window part way and I could smell a change in the air and see it in the sun trying to peek through. I climbed higher the farther south I traveled. Maybe the best thing to do was to keep going and hope I recognized something.

Mentally, I formed a picture of Darwin hefting a pitchfork of mulch, sweat running down his forehead from under a cap he'd mended with duct tape. He enjoyed the outdoors and looked appealing to me when he was involved in his work like that. If Darwin could smile more, he'd be kind of good looking.

One time I was in a treatment team meeting where a long discussion took place about one of our People who wore the same old engineer's cap day in and day out. We work outcome-based programs and decided that an outcome for Jerry would be to get him to switch to a baseball cap and then gradually ratchet him down to wearing it only outdoors. Darwin's cap was a little unusual, but wearing it wasn't a compulsion or anything. I was glad we didn't have to work on that outcome for him.

The road took another unexpected turn. With a start I recognized a familiar-looking township road veering into the woods. A brown sign with yellow lettering carved into it showed I was at the border of Stony Ridge State Park. As I drove by, a little less lost, I remembered my friend and confidante Rhonda Kinder. The cabin we'd stayed in the previous spring wasn't far from there. I could almost hear her exhorting me: "Enjoy the journey, but choose your path with care."

I wondered what Rhonda would think of this path I was on now. It might not be the straight and narrow. Maybe zigzagging. Meeting Darwin. I knew what Barbara Delaney would think. Clinical directors don't approve of socializing with clients. Now, Rhonda would have a different way. She'd always told me to move forward, follow my instincts, take the next step, drive to the next crossroad, examine what I'm seeing. Feel every feeling. Feel lost, even anxious.

As I thought of Reverend Rhonda, a church appeared just ahead, as if on cue. I'd landed in Jericho, another town with a religious-sounding name. I was more familiar with Salem and Zion. They're all similar, just a handful of buildings, a pizza take-out place, a video store, and a gas station reinvented as an auto-body shop. The church roof didn't have enough pitch to look good with a steeple, but had one anyway. Out front, a portable sign with black, slide-in letters announced the sermon title: The Power of Change. "Yeah, right," I muttered under my breath.

2

IN OUR OFFICE, when we do intake we always start with particulars, so here are mine: Name: Angie Halstead; age: forty-two; height: five-foot-two; weight: more than I'd like to say. I'm plain vanilla, brown hair with a bit of gray mixed in; my nose is too wide and has a bump on it (it's not my best feature). I regard myself as friendly, but know sometimes I'm too melancholy and don't smile enough to make me seem approachable. In that way, I guess I'm like Darwin.

The church sign, with its telling sermon title, made me think of Darwin again. He had the power of change. Yes, really. The other day I'd picked him up for one of his appointments and he'd sidetracked us. I shouldn't have humored him, but I did.

"Where exactly is the *park,* of Park Street?" I'd asked to make conversation.

"The park? Oh, I can show you. Do we have time? I bet you never even seen this place." Darwin brightened at the prospect of being my tour guide. Usually it worked the other way.

"Just head down to the railroad and, instead of turning left, where the road takes that sharp bend, go straight. Right here!" Darwin adjusted his cap over his forehead.

"When you come to a fork in the road, take it," I joked weakly.

We scraped bottom on a deep pothole and continued around the bend. I parked under a hefty tulip poplar. "It's a nature preserve owned by the city," he said. "Might be part of the Trail, the old railroad, that is."

Darwin got out of the car and lit a cigarette. A cable strung on low posts marked the picnic area, and he plunked down on the only bench to smoke. I wanted to remind him not to. It was forest-fire season. But I didn't bother.

I watched as Darwin groped for a coffee can that was sitting under the bench—the familiar ashtray substitute. Every group home has a collection of coffee cans on the front porch, half filled with sand and butts.

Darwin tried to lift the can but it didn't budge.

"Hey," he exclaimed. Then he stood up and carefully rested his cigarette on the edge of the bench. "Look at this!"

"What is it?" I asked nonchalantly.

With Darwin, excitement over a coffee can full of anything didn't surprise me. He was a hunter-gatherer, that's for sure. I'd never known anyone with such a fascination for things most of us would walk past without a second look. But that was Darwin for you. Obsessive-compulsive tendencies.

The can was half full of loose change. We dumped it out onto the ground. Me and Darwin were kneeling there, our heads almost touching, sorting out the coins. I was so aware of him—overly conscious.

Darwin scooped all the change into his backpack. I told him we should report it to the park district, but he kept it. It bought him a carton of cigarettes.

℃

I smiled again with the memory and kept driving, more lost than ever. I tried to imagine the words of the sermon I'd never hear—The Power of Change—as I crested the next hill.

"Yes, no doubt about it," I told myself, "I'm lost." About then I caught a glimpse of what I thought might be Wine Creek. I'd recognize that. It would wind its way through Stony Ridge State Park somewhere, so I couldn't be too far away.

It seemed longer ago when I thought of it, but it had been just last spring that we women—we called ourselves Sister Source—camped together for a weekend in Stony Ridge. That's when I'd first met Rhonda. I still remember the coltsfoot and fiddlehead fern, and the giant Allegheny mound ants. That day I had seen my first red-tailed hawk. The first I'd ever noticed, at least.

Wine Creek led me around a lot of unfamiliar curves until I emerged into farmland once more. The fields had those round hay bales scattered over them. They made odd shadows across the landscape. And every lane had a mailbox with a red flag. Pretty scenery, but not the road I needed. Then, just when I thought I'd driven into Pennsylvania, I saw a sign for Old Route 30, the Lincoln Highway just ahead. What a relief!

That was when I pulled over into a lane that led to an oil well and finally retrieved a map from my trunk. It was one an agency worker had given to me. Said it has every road in the county on it, but by then I was off the map.

I felt stupid, and worried too. I didn't have much to go on and would have to stop somewhere and ask. I began to worry about finding Darwin and the farm—I'd been calling it Mel's Garlic Farm—while it was still daylight. The days were getting noticeably shorter this time of year. I worried that Darwin was worrying about me.

I went to the trunk again, hoping to find a better map. I was grateful I'd unloaded the newspapers and aluminum cans. My trunk was as full as my People's vehicles, only more organized. We all have so much stuff. Backpack, water bottles, duffle bag—even a tote with wheels. I pushed aside the bundle of grocery bags I'd meant to drop off at the food co-op and rummaged again in a plastic bin where I kept my eclectic collection of "car junk"—stuff I didn't want to carry in my purse, which I was trying not to weigh down on account of my sore shoulder.

I grabbed a protein bar from my gym bag and took inventory: running shoes, sweat suit, shorts, toiletries, a brush with a folding handle. I was compulsive about going to the gym. I'm prepared for anything, I decided. Almost anything.

On the map I noted the burg I'd need to watch for. From there it looked to be another six miles or so. Darwin and Mel had all the garlic planted by that time, I was sure. Now I was just hoping to get there before dark.

To still the voices in my head, I popped one of Rhonda's tapes in, wishing again I could afford a new car with a CD player. Rhonda had given me her old tape collection when her car-salesman husband bought her a new minivan. Listening to her music made me feel happier.

"Rhonda," I whispered to the windshield, "I'm going to Mel's Garlic Farm. What do you think about that?" Her music seemed to answer.

> What is this place where we are meeting?
> Only a house, the earth its floor.
> Walls and a roof, sheltering people
> Windows for light, an open door.
> Yet it becomes a body that lives
> When we are gathered here
> And know our God is near.

This surprised me, but I tried to pay attention. "Rhonda," I told her. "You are going to have to help me find my way. I am just so lost right now, but I can't turn back."

I spied a woman gathering clothes off the line in the murky evening light. I wondered how it would feel to live there. I suddenly craved the dim natural light coming through a window in late afternoon instead of the harsh fluorescents at the gym. An open door instead of air-conditioning. A real fire for heat. A fire like Rhonda built that night we stayed at the cabin. Floors made of planks, bricks, stones. And people telling stories.

"Rhonda," I said to the windshield, "I would like to paint a picture of that woman at the clothesline. I'd like to catch that dull light in the sky and that other light in her window."

Rhonda was silent. But at that exact moment, a red-tail swooped into my path. I heard his cry as he soared back up and over a pasture, and I craned my neck to follow the arc. But he and Rhonda were gone too quickly, leaving me on my own with my questions.

Rhonda was my holy listener. We still met once a month and she listened to me talk about my life, just as she had that first day in Stony Ridge. Her responses outlined my growing edges. She'd say, "Pay attention to that" or "Stay with that feeling" or "Be grateful for that."

Sometimes I'd thought she knew things about me I didn't know. "Muscles have memory," she'd say to me when I mentioned my aching shoulder.

My muscles remembered harsh words: You should have known better. What were you thinking? What's the matter with you? You deserve to get hurt if you're going to do something that stupid!

I told Rhonda that once. Then I started crying. Rhonda just nodded and handed me a tissue.

The Church of the Crucified Redeemer, where Rhonda was pastor, wasn't the most inviting-looking house of worship—nothing like the white-steepled country churches I noticed that day on my way to meet Darwin. It sat wedged between Rocky's Video Arcade and Mama Rosa's Pizzeria. In the storefront was a selection of sickly greenery backed by a homemade yellow, double-knit curtain. Center stage was a Styrofoam cross, surrounded by perpetual plastic lilies and a basket of fake roses of every color. The whole random arrangement was propped on a box draped with a burgundy lace tablecloth. Static-cling letters on the window proclaimed, "Welcome Everyone! Sunday Worship 11 a.m. Saturday Seekers 7 p.m."

It wasn't the front window, but it might have been the coffee that attracted me at first. That and the singing. The coffee was Equal Exchange Organic, fairly traded, and when I drank it I knew I was helping a poor Central American woman feed her family. Saturday Seekers was supposed to be for people who were afraid of religion. Religion, it turned out, wasn't what any of us wanted. We were all women and what we wanted was something I'd call spirituality, a nurturing and exploring of the inner life. One evening someone called us Sister Source, and it stuck. So I learned—I'm still learning—to be part of what Rhonda envisioned as a community of faith.

When I was growing up here in Addison County, my family went to a church on the edge of Ebenezer. I entertained myself by making etchings of the lyre embossed on the front of the hymnal.

We had our rituals: sang about Jesus, put money in the offering. Everyone shook the hand of the minister, who flowed down the aisle at the end of the service while the congregation sang "Praise God from Whom All Blessings Flow." Everything seemed to flow together then.

I became part of a community of faith when women with names like Eileen and Lulu Anne called the children up front on our birthdays to put pennies in a special offering while everyone sang to us. Then Eileen pinned a small badge on each of us. I'd tiptoe back to my wooden folding chair and look down at my chest, trying to see the picture on the pin and wishing Sunday school would end so I could look.

When I was twelve we suddenly stopped going to that church. One afternoon that year Mom attended Quaker Meeting. She had many friends back then, as she still does. She liked Meeting, where there was no singing or preaching, just silence. A lanky guy in horn-rimmed glasses stood up that day, eyes blazing with the Inner Light that Quakers are so famous for. He talked for a full thirty minutes in protest of the Vietnam War.

When you're a Quaker, such views are expected. What wasn't expected was the effect the Quaker's "witness" had on my mom. She went home and wrote a letter to the editor of the local daily newspaper, *The Repositor*. Without talking to anyone, never waiting to let it cool, she sealed the envelope, walked to the mailbox, and flipped up the red flag for the mailman.

Two days later the letter—her first to an editor—was published. Her name appeared in bold, black letters at the exact bottom center of the Letters page. That same afternoon our tough-minded, straight-laced minister called my mother and asked her to stop by the parsonage office. She thought he wanted to talk about the Ladies Mission

Society. But two deacons were already seated in the living room when she arrived. They stood politely, but the grim look on the face of the reverend's wife as she handed Mom a china cup of coffee, into which cream had already been poured, signaled the gravity of the moment.

I could imagine the way she sank down on the sofa, methodically placing the teacup full of tepid coffee on the nearby table. But when she heard what the reverend and his deacons had to say, she pulled herself up to her full five foot, two inches. She looked that starchy preacher in the eye, her newfound political voice shaking and raw, and restated the views of her letter. The Bible she read didn't condone the bombing of Southeast Asian peasants, she told him.

I could imagine how she must have looked there in the parsonage, in a homemade blue-flowered dress and a white cardigan. How she must have brought her slight body off the sofa, stood ramrod straight, and lifted her chin to face the three men in front of her. I can hear the steely sound of her voice as she asked the preacher to remove her name from the membership roll. She must have almost marched to the front door in her low-heeled pumps, leaving the coffee untouched and quivering on the table.

That day a political activist was born. Later I wondered why she indulged that sudden impulse after years of one routine. I was young and unaware of what was going on inside her at the time. Eventually I started asking myself how she did it. How did she find the courage to speak out? As I drove past those gravel-covered lanes and white mail-boxes, some with their flags up and some with them down, I thought about my mom, who found her voice and lost her religion all in one day.

She never changed her hairstyle. The French twist went from gray to white. She just bought bobby pins to blend in.

Three decades later, she still wore a white cardigan sweater and ordered summer cotton dresses from a New England mail-order catalog. In late fall she changed to elastic-waist, twill slacks and embroidery-trimmed knit shirts. And she'd never been afraid to speak out—politically or otherwise—since.

As I drove I remembered she was off in Honduras on her latest medical mission trip. I admired what she did, but I stayed here, working for social justice at Helping Hands.

After that fateful day, I went with Mom to Quaker Meeting. I wish I could tell you that our family was better off for having endured this heroic passage of my mother, but for years we all felt the loss. Dad never understood Mom's sudden protest. He didn't share her sentiments but kept his resentment mostly to himself and became more quiet and aloof.

The letter and all the upheaval that followed hurt his agricultural sales business. Maybe a quiet revolution took place inside him too, because after years of selling pesticides and chemical fertilizers, he became a soil tester and a distributor for Natural Farm Organics. I followed him too, in another way, out onto the farms and into the fields, where I learned to love the landscape. Back then I took in everything I saw out there, and when I wasn't allowed to ride along with Dad, I tried to paint the landscape with a watercolor set I'd bought at the five-and-dime.

In place of familiar religious rituals, I learned to accept the unexpected. I stared unseeingly at the cheap knotty-pine paneling behind the lectern while some smooth-headed man with a beard or an obese woman in a caftan talked about the atomic bomb or the KKK or how to get more voters registered in Alabama.

I didn't understand much of any of that back then, but out in the parking lot after meeting, I'd always follow the caftan. She'd reach into the voluminous folds and pull out a couple of orange-flavor marshmallow circus peanuts or a handful of fat peppermints that tasted like Pepto Bismol. I was too old to be begging for candy, so she'd sneak them to me in a way that made me think we were the only two who knew. And maybe we were. I sucked on that sweetness in the back seat on the way home, my eyes drinking in the view as I indulged in my own childhood rituals.

3

"TAKE THE SECOND ROAD to the left after Fieldstone Road and go for 6.3 miles." I was amused by the precision of Darwin's written directions. "You will come to a bend in the road and a small shed near the ditch. After the bend there is a driveway with the number 22530 on the mailbox. Make a sharp right onto the lane. It's a steep hill, so keep your car in first gear and go at least twenty miles per hour to make it up the driveway. Watch for some big stones and a washout, if it's wet. At the top of the hill, you'll see the house." I had a fleeting thought of Darwin and the marked-up map in his Louis L'Amour paperback.

Ascending the lane, the reason for Darwin's precision was clear. My heart pounded as I lurched forward, poised to shift into second, if necessary. Dusk had left quickly and under the trees that lined the lane it was incredibly dark. I was bewildered by my foolishness. What was I doing here? Why did I ever agree to this? And why did I keep going when I might have turned around? "Deliver me from evil," I prayed irreverently.

I parked the car and pulled the parking brake harder than necessary, wrenching my sore shoulder in the process. I sat there a moment feeling that something new, large, and unknown was just ahead, and I was afraid. It wasn't a fear for physical safety, but had something to do with entering a new and lonely place I didn't fully understand. I'd taken a huge risk both personally and professionally.

I'd overstepped a boundary and hadn't begun to calculate the cost of my actions.

I approached a dim light at the door of the farmhouse and picked my way up the porch steps, kicking into a well-chewed dog bone before I knocked on the screen door. Behind the screen I could see the peeling, wooden panel door, and then I heard a large dog bark. The man who came to the door wasn't Darwin. In truth, I hadn't expected Darwin to answer the door. But I was pretty sure I was at the right place.

"Well, well," said the man roughly. "Our traveler has arrived. Aren't you a little late? We gave up on you long ago. 'Specially Darwin. I take it you're Angie?"

Darwin was standing behind the man, whom I assumed to be his uncle Mel, in the shadows. They looked tired. From his records, I knew Darwin was forty-five. Mel was just slightly older, I guessed, and I was surprised to imagine that nephew and uncle were about the same age.

"Angel, I didn't think you were coming. Thought you'd chickened out."

"Oh, I'm so sorry. I got lost. I meant to be here long ago."

"Well, don't just stand there," Uncle Mel said. "You might as well come on in now that you're here."

In the shadows I quickly took in Mel's ruddy complexion, visible even in the dim light. His hair was that short, nondescript, farmer-boy style, shaved close up the back with a thick, blond forelock slicked back from a side part. Now I was completely inside the door and immediately caught a whiff of the farm, no doubt coming from a pair of dirty Wellingtons resting on a plastic mat.

"Well, Angie, you missed planting garlic today," Mel said.

"Oh, I know. I wanted to get here to help. Darwin told me to come early. I left Hilldale this morning, thinking it would be easy to find you. But then the day got away. I should know better. I have a terrible sense of direction. I finally remembered a map in my trunk, or I'd probably be in West Virginia by now."

It was a curious thing, but after leaving Hilldale when I went to college, I'd lived in large cities for more than a decade. Long enough, anyway, to make me aware of the lack of ordinary courtesies here. People were truly friendly underneath. It was just that introductions weren't real important most of the time. So there I was, wondering what to do about meeting Darwin's uncle.

"You're Mel, I take it? Darwin's uncle Mel?"

"That's me," he said extending his hand. "Mel Martin."

Again I felt unsure of etiquette. The woman is supposed to extend her hand first.

"Pleased to meet you, Mel Martin," I replied. His hand wasn't like the hands I was used to shaking. It was rough and thick. The handshake was firm and came from his shoulder, as if he were grasping a pump handle.

We stood there making small talk inside the front door and I let my eyes adjust. Finally Darwin wandered over to a sofa and Mel followed.

Without invitation, I sank into a worn, over-stuffed chair that seemed to fit my body perfectly. I was starting to feel a bit more at home. I studied Darwin's uncle with a practiced, professional eye, as if he were a new consumer assigned to my caseload. Darwin yawned and reached for a magazine, then laid it aside.

"Well, well, well. So here's the famous Angel girl," Mel said in a mocking way that bothered me. "Dar' told me how you got him that job. Stroke of genius on your part,

I'd say. Getting him out of the house doing something productive for a change."

I didn't like the hint of judgment I heard in his statement, and I felt defensive. He had no idea what a struggle it was for Darwin just to get out of bed and care for his basic needs.

"Darwin is doing quite well at Farnswalters," I said, maintaining my professional demeanor in spite of the fact it was Saturday evening. "We are so pleased with his progress." I knew I needed to include Darwin in this conversation about himself.

"How do you like that job by now?" I asked, turning toward him.

"It's a job. . . . Better than pulling Brooms and Buckets," he said, referring to Helping Hands' abandoned janitorial service.

"Darwin is making a lot of progress and we are so pleased he could get in there. Our vocational staff work hard to find the right employee-employer match." I was suddenly aware that my stuffy social-worker language seemed out of place in the relaxed farmhouse.

"Good, good. You get him fixed up and maybe I can get more help out of him here. This place is almost too much for one guy to handle." Mel obviously wanted to change the subject, and so did I.

"How many acres do you have here?" That's a safe question to ask a farmer, but the longer I sat there, the more questions I had. It was obvious there hadn't been a woman's touch in the house for a long time, yet there were suggestions that someone once lived there, someone who had placed hand-crocheted doilies on the back of an easy chair and bought a floor lamp with a ruffled shade.

"I couldn't make it without the help of Dad and Paulie, my brother. Dad comes over most evenings to help with the milking and we all three do the field work of two farms. This is the homeplace here," Mel divulged. "It was getting to be too much for Mom and Dad, so when I moved back they bought a place in town and I took things over. We don't have a big herd, as far as that goes. Just about thirty cows and a bunch of heifers, of course."

This is the homeplace. I heard the words and let them settle.

"Don't forget the horses," Darwin said.

"Oh, yes, well, they're just for fun. You gotta have some fun."

In the dim light through a double doorway I noticed bookshelves packed full and spilling over onto the surrounding floor. There was an old wooden desk with tarnished brass drawer pulls and overflowing plastic milk crates filled with notebooks and journals. In spite of the fact that there were three or four lamps in the room, we sat in the glow of one weak overhead light—the kind you'd normally find on a bedroom ceiling. It was way too dark for my tastes.

"Well, speaking of cows, we need to hit the hay," Mel said glancing at the clock ticking away the seconds on the opposite wall.

I felt alarmed, wondering how I'd manage to drive all the way back after dark when I'd barely found my way there in the daylight. Mel must have seen the anxiety on my face.

"It's way too late to drive back tonight," he said brusquely. "Particularly if you are directionally challenged."

Everything about this man surprised me; the "directionally challenged" comment didn't seem natural coming from someone who lived in an old-fashioned house.

"I know it's late. I'm so sorry to barge in like this. I should have just turned around and headed back when I finally figured out where I was."

"No way!" exclaimed Darwin. "You're here now. Just stay over."

"You shouldn't go back tonight," Mel agreed. "It's getting late and some of those roads are just one pothole after another. You might sink into one of them and never be seen again. Stay over, and Darwin can go back with you tomorrow. It's Sunday, but I'll stay home from church. Mom will call to find out where I was, but you're a good enough excuse to stay home one Sunday."

I was beginning to feel better about Mel, whether because of the idea he went to church or because of the long speech that seemed kinder than his first comments.

"If you stay over, you can save me a trip tomorrow to take Darwin back. That way I don't have to drive him home and find someone to chore for me again. We shoulda fixed up that old car of his, but I guess there for a while he was in no shape to drive anyway."

"Yeah," I replied. "It seemed right at the time, at least. But I don't want to put you out. Are you sure its okay? I do have some stuff in my car—my gym bag. That would probably get me through the night."

"Well, then we're settled," Mel said.

I glanced at the rotary telephone on the old gossip bench. I hadn't seen one of those in years. There was a pile of out-dated phone directories, and the whole set-up looked intimidating. I briefly considered calling someone, but Mom was gone—thank goodness—on another one of her cross-cultural crusades. We kept track of one another, maybe something like Mel and his mother. If I'd called mine, nothing I said about my whereabouts would make sense. It didn't even make sense to *me*.

We trekked out to the car to retrieve my bag, all of us: me, Darwin, Mel with a flashlight, and Buster, Mel's non-descript farm dog. Then they showed me to my room.

"Tomorrow's another day," Mel said redundantly before he wandered off to the stairway door.

"Well, yes. I suppose it is."

Darwin hung around, leaning on the doorframe. He put his foot up on the old blanket chest inside the door and tightened his shoelace. I recognized the gesture for what it was. He was stalling, hoping for some kindness from his Angel. I was feeling the first of many twinges of remorse for what I'd done. My unprofessional conduct could very well make all our lives more difficult. I was worried about what it was going to mean for Darwin—and for me as his case manager—'er, resource manager.

Darwin looked like he might hug me. Or like he wanted to. He searched my face for some sign we'd moved to a different place in our relationship, beyond a care-taking-needy-disabled-person twosome to something more interesting. But I gave him no reason for hope.

"Are you doing okay with those meds still?" I asked in my best case-manager voice. "I'm glad you can come here on weekends. Your uncle Mel seems like a fine person who could provide you with some excellent support. Supportive family members are a real key to recovery from a mental illness, you know. You are lucky to have him."

Darwin got my message and nodded. I saw the familiar melancholy return to his face. I didn't think a lot about it at the time or about how my own neediness was masked by the professionalism. If I had seen something on his face, I'd have labeled it some variation of "flat affect," that characteristic lack of animation and facial mobility so common among my People. As for me, I would say I was overly tired. But then, it was getting late and I was lost in the dark.

4

FROM THE BEDROOM WINDOW next morning, I caught my first glimpse of one of the best-kept, most beautiful farms I'd ever seen. It cascaded across the rolling hills, and I felt as if I were seeing it all from the highest point in the county. I smelled cows and heard a rooster crowing, defying the myth that roosters only crow at dawn—it was long past daybreak.

The house was deserted. It was small by farmhouse standards and the mix of functional furnishings spanned several generations. Cast-iron radiators had useful little shelves built over them, and in the bathroom one incorporated a towel bar to supply a warm towel after my shower.

The coffee simmering on the back of the stove was bitter by the time I poured mine. A huge Mason jar of homemade cereal and a ripe banana, all speckled and sweet, were strategically placed beside an empty cereal bowl by someone—probably Darwin trying to be my benefactor. I found a pitcher of raw milk in the fridge.

The screen door slammed, and Mel entered and removed his boots. He walked softly across the kitchen in his socks and pulled out one of the earliest specimens of chair planted around the table. He took a small, hardcover book from the pocket of his coveralls. "Darwin's still feeding," he told me, dropping his farm cap that advertised some unknown farm product.

He started reading *Leaves of Grass*, but then seemed to realize it might be impolite. There were plenty of things I wanted to ask him, but I was at a loss for words. I carefully sorted through the common conversational stepping-stones: How many years have you lived here? What do you grow besides garlic?

My other questions would wait awhile. They were the ones I wondered about the most. Were you ever married? How are you related to Darwin? Now *that* was a question I could ask! It's always a good idea to find out how people are related. You can learn a lot about them in a hurry, especially if you discover you're second cousins once removed on your mother's side.

Mel told me he'd been married to Darwin's mother's sister, Loretta, but she had died suddenly the same year they'd taken over the farm, soon after Mel's parents retired. Loretta died of a blood clot, following minor surgery. I would have liked to know more about her, but just nodded in a way I hoped communicated sympathy. Mel got quiet again. My one question had provided answers for the others, so I asked about *Leaves of Grass*.

Our conversation took us to the bookshelf, and Mel moved the messy boxes of journals and notebooks aside for a tour of his reading habits. Suddenly he seemed more animated. He liked classics. American authors. Nature. History. Modern fiction. He had a collection of field guides and the standby literary classics of a nature lover: Thoreau, Annie Dillard, John Muir, Rachel Carson. There was a shelf beside his desk filled with technical manuals and stacks of thick, black notebooks overflowing with clippings from journals and obscure newsletters. But before I could ask about them, Mel was asking me questions.

He pumped me for more information about Darwin's illness.

"After Aunt Alice died, Darwin just sort of lost it," Mel said.

"We've been working together for a few months now,"

I hedged, feeling uncomfortable with where the conversation was going. I didn't like talking to relatives without a signed consent form and didn't remember Darwin giving permission. Still, it seemed they were very close and Darwin *had* invited me here. We weren't in a mental health center; we were on the homeplace, as my host had called it.

"Jeez, he was a nut case back then," Mel said.

"That's not the official diagnosis," I said.

"A crisis of any serious nature can exacerbate the depressive disorder. Then we see mania—the psychotic features. Untreated, it can lead to a suicide attempt and hospitalization, as you saw with Darwin. Thank goodness he wasn't successful and got help in time."

I tried to talk in generalities, but I hated the way I sounded.

"My mom was just doing her usual Mennonite thing and took him a chicken noodle casserole, rhubarb pie, and who knows what else," Mel said.

"I know. She was trying to help. For most people that would be a great thing to do. But by that time he'd lost his ability for rational thought. We found out he hadn't slept for several nights—or days. That's an indicator of serious mood problems too."

I shifted the conversation to a topic that wouldn't compromise my ethics. "But enough of that. Your folks are Mennonite? Does that mean you are too?"

"Yeah, I guess you could say that. If they haven't disowned me yet." Mel dropped his eyes. "But, anyway, when Mom showed up on his doorstep, Darwin just went totally ballistic. Dad took matters into his own hands that day, I'm afraid. He admits he lost his temper, but then after he left, he stopped at a gas station and called the hotline. Mom was upset about that too. Didn't think he should have."

"Well, really, it was the best thing," I said, trying to be

reassuring. "Early treatment is the key, and the problems were probably brewing long before they erupted in front of your folks that day."

"He got so depressed after his mother passed away. He always was kind of a weird bird anyhow. I never understood why he sifts through other people's garbage. That's just so embarrassing to the family. We just swept it under the rug as long as we could. But he seems a lot better lately. Probably thanks to you." Mel gave me a shy glance and fiddled with the pages of his book.

"The DBT group—that stands for dialectal behavior therapy—really helps some of our People. And then we have the Clubhouse for socialization skills, and some of the more high-functioning People like Darwin get into the supportive job training and skills enhancement program. We work hard with this job-readiness training. It's one of our newest programs." Mel looked at me with eyebrows raised, and I realized again I was speaking social-work lingo. But I couldn't stop myself.

"Helping Hands is the behavioral-health authority for the county's SMD population, you know."

"SMD? Now you're definitely out of my league," Mel remarked.

"Severely mentally disabled. I know it's not a nice-sounding label, but it does provide the ticket for all these services under the government guidelines and it's a godsend for a lot of folks." I looked at Mel, hoping he appreciated the help we'd given his nephew.

Maybe the conversation wasn't going as well as I'd hoped. But we had connected easily, and I was beginning to feel very comfortable with Mel.

I gave him a medium-sized version of my job description as we stood watching Darwin. He'd finished the chores and was cleaning up the garden.

"Good my mom isn't here to see this," Mel said. "She'd never approve of Darwin working in the garden on Sunday."

I smiled, thinking of my own habit of doing housework on the Sabbath and how I was feeling less and less unrighteous as the years went by. Darwin yanked on the sweet-corn stalks. It was high time to pull the brittle bean vines and hack off the stalks. The tomato and squash vines would stay till after the frost. He stopped every so often and wandered away, probably to smoke. Then he'd come back and start in again. Mel left on some chore while I washed the dishes in the sink before stepping out on the porch.

č

Looking across the fields, I felt the familiar mixture of anxiety and oppressive yearning rise inside me. It was coming more often. There was no logical explanation for it. By all accounts I should have been happy, especially in this beautiful place. But something was wrong. Even taking into account my little indiscretion and violation of consumer-social worker boundaries, there was just something wrong inside me and I couldn't figure it out—or didn't want to just yet. Earlier I'd thought this visit was the cause of my dis-ease. Now I wondered if Mel's homeplace was the real reason I felt such discontent.

I probably hadn't been on a farm since I was a little girl. Many of the farms in our area were being swallowed up by shopping malls or housing developments, or being consumed by some large-scale farmer who thought he could beat the system by operating on a grander scale, building a large hog or veal barn or planting only corn and soybeans year after year. Mel's small dairy farm was almost the exception. But the further you got from Hilldale, the more likely you were to see the old-fashioned farms I remembered from childhood.

I used to ride out into the country with my father to call on his customers. We'd poke our heads in the out-buildings, and I'd catch a whiff of dust—an aroma of things foreign to me, yet so common: piles of mowed grasses rotting under pine trees, ancient axle grease coating the sills of machinery sheds, ears of corn resting in their cribs, and apples moldering under the tree, tempting the groundhog that lived under its roots. Now, once again all my senses were coming alive at once. The melancholy mood hovered in the air around me like a cloud.

Suddenly Mel came running, yelling for Darwin. "Come, help! We're missing six head. Looks like they broke through at the back of the pasture near that low spot. Let's go get 'em!"

Mel was breathing hard, as if he'd run the whole way from the back of the pasture. His red hanky was flapping out of his jeans pocket. He clutched a hammer and a hand-ful of U-shaped nails.

"I need a couple of cowhands. Right now!" Mel shouted.

Darwin ran from where he'd been chopping down stalks. "Where'd they head for?" he asked.

"Don't know. Looks like they could have gone across the crick. Could be anywhere: out on the road, over at the Granger Place, even down the gorge."

"You go on the road around to the Grangers'. I'll head back to the fence. Maybe I can track them from there. If you see 'em, holler."

Mel shouted his instructions to both of us as he took off toward the pasture, leaving Darwin to teach me every-thing he knew about heifer herding in one easy lesson.

I grabbed my shoes and let the screen door slam.

Darwin started up a four-wheeler and pulled away almost before I could climb on the seat behind him. I craned my neck as we rounded the bend and headed down the steep lane. I stretched to see the neighbor's cornfield as I steadied myself.

"Is that them over there?" I shouted above the roar. Darwin bounced the vehicle over a large boulder sticking through the gravel. I flew off the seat but caught myself by grabbing onto his waist. We plummeted down the lane at breathtaking speed.

He veered off before necessary, through the ditch and out over the wheat stubble. I strained my eyes looking for the black and white bodies of the strays that might be just over the next hill. Sure enough, there was a Holstein at the edge of the Grangers' cornfield. Darwin revved up the motor and raced toward the animals.

I wanted to tell him to slow down, but it was too late. The animals heard him coming and ran, tails high in the air, toward the road—exactly the wrong way.

"Dang! What the . . .?" Darwin swore under his breath and kept chasing them.

The next thing I knew, we were bouncing toward the road with six heifers running six directions in front of the four-wheeler. I saw from there that if we got them safely across the road, we could run them down the fencerow in the gully and through the gate at the back of the pasture. Darwin took the road ditch with a flying leap. Fortunately for us, nothing was coming, but the stray herd wasn't cooperating.

On impulse, I jumped off the four-wheeler and ran toward the leader, shooing her away from the corn and toward the gully. Even *I* knew we didn't want cows in the neighbor's corn.

"Hee-aww!" I yelled as I ran across the stubble,

waving my arms. My ankle twisted in my flat, city-girl loafers. The stubble cut into my bare legs, leaving red scratches. But my quick thinking paid off, and the herd leader ran down the bank to the gully. Darwin finally cut the engine and watched as I raced after the others in turn. We herded them down the fencerow until we reached Mel coming toward us. Darwin revved up and took off again like a shot, leaving me to return on foot.

The heifers were headed back up the gully, and Mel shouted at Darwin and me, waving the hammer over his head. Two strays trampled the corn at the back of the Grangers' field, and all of us were exhausted when we finally got the heifers back in their own pasture. We collapsed on the porch.

Mel had a cold, sullen look in his eyes. "Darwin, don't you have any sense? You'd do a lot better if you'd just rounded up the herd on foot. The last thing strays need is a loud four-wheeler chasing them into the cornfield. You need to get off your butt and do a little real work for a change."

I winced for Darwin. I didn't like this side of Mel, but had to admit Darwin's lack of judgment bothered me too.

Darwin leaned down to untie his work boots and I saw the tension rising in him. He was struggling for control. "What do you know, you shit-kickin' wise ass? Who made you the big boss man anyway?" I covered my ears while their tempers flared higher.

Mel turned away in silence, and Darwin kicked his boots off. They landed with a thud in the dry ground beside the hydrangea bush, where they remained under the blue blossoms, later reminding me of the painful scene.

I felt the tension and followed Mel into the house while Darwin walked the other direction, reaching for his smokes. My host went to the kitchen sink to wash up and then pulled out a chopping board and a heavy knife. He was starting dinner—the noon meal on a farm. Mel began by cooking a pan of rice. Then he minced three thumb-sized cloves of garlic. I stood at the sink, cleaning the vegetables he'd given me for the stir-fry he was cooking and listening into the silence for a clue about Darwin's whereabouts, but I heard nothing. Mel chopped with a vengeance, and I felt fragile and strange, caught like a heifer in their disagreement.

Mel pulled a well-seasoned wok and large, wooden cooking tools from a shelf above the gas range and poured a little oil in the hot, black well. He quickly added the garlic and vegetables one at a time.

Darwin came in looking discouraged. I gave him a kind smile, but he barely looked up as he sat at the kitchen table and read *Farming Magazine* while he waited for Mel's dinner.

"Mel, what is this?" I asked, looking in a pot, partly to break the awkward silence.

"Well, for sure not that sixty-second rice. What do people eat with that rice, anyway? It only takes twenty minutes to steam rice. Just the time needed to cook a decent stir-fry."

Mel's perfect rice was topped with a fabulous concoction of garlic, beef, and fresh celery, onions, and peppers from the garden. At the last he tossed in a pint of cherry tomatoes Darwin had picked from the vines behind the house. The pungent smell of Southeast Asian fish sauce reminded me there were still things about Mel I needed to know. Where did he learn to cook with something like that?

I fumbled with the chopsticks propped on the edge of my large dinner plate, and Mel finally had mercy and reached behind him in a drawer to get forks for Darwin and me. We ate without saying much. Mel tried to smooth things between himself and Darwin in that way men have of not really apologizing but signaling they want to let bygones be bygones.

"Gotta check that fence a little better one of these days," he said, thinking out loud. "I could've lost one of them heifers on the road."

"Yeah," Darwin muttered, "I can check it next weekend, if you can wait."

The conversation frittered away as both of them realized it was leading, without meaning to, right back to another ride on the four-wheeler. None of us wanted to go *there*.

Darwin and I cleaned up, and Mel carried the vegetable peelings to the compost pile. I watched him turn the rich compost with a pitchfork. His biceps bulged under his limp T-shirt, and I wished once more I'd been there to help plant the fall garden. At dinner he had said, "Folks here called a garden like that a truck patch. You plant enough to sell and take it to town in a truck." Mel stooped to inspect the tilth of the soil where the day before he and Darwin had planted ten pounds of garlic at the edge of the big garden.

"Growing garlic takes patience," he told me. "You save the dry bulbs from last year and in October you break them apart. You grow it in the fine soil from the bottom of the compost pile." There I was, seeing the actual compost he was talking about.

"We sprinkled a wheelbarrow full of manure into the patch too," he said. "Garlic stays in the ground all winter in Ohio. Between now and the first hard frost, one shoot comes up. The frost will kill off the stalks and through the winter the plant lies dormant, waiting for the warmth of spring. Then the bulb will send up a new shoot."

At times, I had a sense that there was hidden meaning in his words. It was as if he was telling me something about life. Maybe about my life, or his own. Or perhaps even Darwin's life. We were all starting a life cycle, and it was a beginning time of something yet to come.

"Growers here pinch the tops to make sure the stem doesn't form a head, that way the nutrients go under-ground to feed the new garlic bulb."

Darwin and Mel sat on the porch with me and told me about the garlic festival held after harvest season the year before. I felt more hopeful for the two of them then. The anger seemed to have gone as quickly as it had come.

"The festival is a great place to find new varieties," Mel said. "We tasted garlic from all over the country. Yesterday we planted Music and Romanian Red."

"Awfully nice names for such a stinky crop," I said, trying to imagine socializing with people tasting garlic at a festival.

C

By then I was tired, my ankle ached and the scratches still stung. I hadn't tended to them. I wanted to tell Mel a thing or two about the way he'd talked to Darwin and to explain what Darwin needed from a family member.

What I was beginning to recognize, though, was the way his farm somehow made me feel weak and vulnerable inside—unless it was Mel who was doing that. I wanted to risk trusting someone again. But the time wasn't right, so we sat there talking about garlic and I tried to forget Mel's harsh—though possibly justified—words to Darwin. I was Darwin's champion and just dimly aware that the incident had stirred something I'd been avoiding.

I thought of Rhonda's recent counsel: "The mind, body, and soul are all connected. The task of the maturing adult is letting go." What to let go of, I wasn't sure. And she didn't say.

"You spend the first half of life building up and gathering," she'd said. "Now you will begin to sort through your acquisitions and let go of all that does not serve you."

"Maybe I should see someone at the clinic for some medicine to help me get through this bad time," I thought as we all sat in silence on the porch that Sunday afternoon. But inside I knew my problem was spiritual, and medicine couldn't fix what was wrong.

5

WHEN I RETURNED to Helping Hands on Monday morning, there were two critical incident reports on the fax machine. They were in my hand when Joe and Erika walked through the door seconds later.

"Good morning, young 'uns!" I greeted them. Both Joe and Erika were under my supervision. We had gotten a lot of recent social-work graduates who came to work at the agency and collect the requisite number of supervised hours, a requirement for licensure.

"What's that?" Joe asked, gesturing toward the sheaf of papers in my hand. He was so new he hadn't seen a CIR yet.

"Come over and have a look. We might as well continue your orientation to the mental-health system right now. These are reports filed by the crisis team or law enforcement informing us of critical incidents that took place over the weekend. Someone will fax the report to us from the hospital or the justice center, depending on the nature of the incident. Looks like we have one of each here."

I glanced at Joe and Erika, who were straining to see the names printed on the papers.

"Let's go into my office and review these." I motioned to the two, and they followed me into my cubicle and perched on the orange, molded-plastic chairs that were too sturdy to leave the office when the shag carpet was replaced in the waiting room.

"It looks as if Mac is back in jail. The report says an officer was called when he threatened someone outside the phone booth at the Starfire station. He assaulted a woman and tore her blouse, then chased her down the street. She escaped but he then climbed a chain-link fence of the Lafayette Welding Company. The night guard turned him in."

"It's too bad," Erika said. "He was doing pretty well last time I saw him, going to AA meetings and staying off the streets. How long will he be in for, do you think?"

"He wasn't taking his medication regularly, remember?" I said. "We have to keep him on it. Otherwise stuff like this is bound to happen. Hard to say how long they'll keep him, but it's not the first offense. Could be a couple of weeks, or longer depending on whether the victim presses charges and the welding company decides to take action against him for trespassing. One thing's for sure: He can't afford an attorney and no one will let him off the hook because he was delusional. He probably has no idea he did all this. The illness took over. Mental illness and alcohol are a disastrous combination. Sad to say, he'll be back to square one if he sits in jail with no medication for several weeks or months."

I glanced at the second report and shuddered. This was one of my People. I spread the first page out in front of my supervisees and pointed to the sketch of a human form with Xs marking physical injury. Kyra Cunningham was a calm person, even complacent. She lived in low-income housing on a narrow street on the lower edge of town.

"I knew Kyra was decompensating," I told the two young case managers. "I just had no idea she was this bad. We were trying to get an early appointment with the psychiatrist for her because it seemed as if a lot of things were making her anxious. I saw signs she was delusional.

I always know something is amiss when she tells me the refrigerator is sending electricity into her kitchen and then refuses to cook meals or clean up her dishes."

"What exactly happened?" asked Joe.

This was a teachable moment for Joe and Erika. I glanced at the clock, trying to gauge how much time I had to educate my new staff members about critical incidents and some of the other realities they would soon face on a more or less regular basis. My mind was spinning as I thought about Kyra and the serious nature of the injuries indicated by the report.

"I guess her family knows what is going on," said Erika.

"Not necessarily," I said. "I can't remember at the moment if Kyra has signed a consent form that would allow the hospital to notify them in an emergency like this. If she doesn't have one on file with us, the weekend staff would have refused to give out any information, even if they tried to find out."

"That is terrible!" exclaimed Erika. "You mean to tell me she might have spent most of the weekend in the hospital without anybody in her family even knowing?"

"We'll check the file in a minute," I reassured her. "If we can, we will certainly call them right away. This is a bit different from the typical psychiatric hospitalization. She's at the medical center and is being treated for physical injuries. But they'll know from her medical tag that she is a psych patient as well as having diabetes."

I studied the report, trying to figure out what had happened. There was a paragraph that appeared to have been hastily typed and signed by Nancy, the on-call crisis worker. Attached to that was a police report. At that moment, I still wasn't sure if Kyra had been the victim of a crime or had inflicted the injuries on herself.

We didn't have a crisis staff, but regular staff rotated shifts to cover weekends, evenings, and holidays. To our credit, we did have a twenty-four-hour hotline. Most times, if the incident happened late at night, we tried just talking to the caller on the phone and then checked in on them the next day. More than you'd imagine, just talking with people can calm them enough to get them through the night.

"Danger to self or others, you know," I said to Joe and Erika. "That's the guiding principle for action during the night or for any sort of involuntary hospitalization.

"In my opinion, one of the worst things that can happen is for someone to have the crisis team come out in the middle of the night. You are both aware by now, I assume, that when you pull weekend crisis duty you will be riding in the cruiser?"

Joe and Erika nodded, and I continued. "I hate the way we do this. There is nothing worse for someone who is psychotic than having law enforcement come flying up the street, sirens screaming, stopping in front of your house—or worse yet, your group home—with lights flashing. Our person is already paranoid, feeling suicidal, or has attempted suicide. All the neighbors wake up and look out the window, and the stigma of mental illness is perpetuated. Not only are you thought of as 'crazy,' 'nuts' or 'whacked out,' you are now also a dangerous criminal in the eyes of your neighbors."

"Movies like *Psycho* and characters like Hannibal Lecter don't help attitudes toward people with schizophrenia either," Joe said.

"Mental illness, or even a suggestion of it, is so often used as a plot device by screen writers," Erika said. "It's an easy way to get some bizarre yet half-believable action into a story, that's for sure."

I was half listening to them while I studied the report, trying to make some sense of it as the interns talked in generalities. I hoped Kyra hadn't had to endure sirens in the middle of the night. The report said the "incident" happened at about two o'clock Sunday morning. I hoped her family knew what was going on.

I read the report aloud for Erika and Joe.

Client was heard screaming by neighbors in the apartment building, who called the police. Apartment found in disarray, client sitting on floor of bedroom closet. Multiple superficial wounds to trunk and extremities including scrapes, scratches, and bruises. A one-inch laceration to left arm required 10 stitches. Patient sustained serious fracture of the left femur and will need surgery before release.

"Whew!" exclaimed Joe under his breath. "What in the world?"

I sighed in disbelief. "It appears Kyra was assaulted by someone who either lives in the apartment building or got in somehow. The building isn't as secure as it might be, but I don't know the motive. The report says the police are investigating.

"At least Kyra's a patient, not an inmate," I said, thinking of Mac. "'Danger to self' will likely land you in the hospital. Danger to others puts you in jail."

"Isn't it true, though, that psychiatric patients are more likely to be the victims of violence than to commit violence?" Erika asked.

"Without a doubt. Good point."

"Either way," Joe said, "they're probably going to end up with caretakers who don't know enough about their condition if it happens to be schizophrenia or bipolar disorder."

"You two are going to make great social workers," I responded to my charges.

"I'll check in on Kyra today at the hospital and see how things are going. Joe, maybe you'd like to follow up with law enforcement and see what we can find out about both of these incidents. I worry that this assault will exacerbate Kyra's already fragile mental state. Maybe we can minimize the effects if we get to her right away and see to it that she is well taken care of." I glanced at my watch and realized I needed to push on.

"Erika, are you set for the day? Any questions or concerns about your caseload before we head out?"

"I think I'm okay. Are we on for the individual supervisory session for tomorrow?"

I looked at my planner and confirmed the time, then dismissed my protégés so I could go see about Kyra. It was urgent I get to Hilldale Medical Center as soon as possible.

I poured coffee into my commuter mug and thought of the strong brew on Mel's back burner. The weekend seemed far away until I remembered the full moon that lit the way home late Sunday night. The vernal equinox and the ancient rhythms of the season had managed to lull me into thinking all was well. Shadows of tree branches and the scent of fourth-cutting hay gave way to quiet streets as Darwin dozed, leaning against the car door. Finally we turned down one last back alley and completed the trip back to this world, where everything was as confused as when we'd left it—if not more so.

The final approach to town through a series of back roads and alleys was my unnecessary attempt to reassure Darwin and myself that no one would know we had spent a weekend together. Case manager and one of her People. I think we both believed no one would ever find out.

℮

Later, at home in my bed, I slept restlessly and was awakened from some unremembered dream. I lay there in the middle of the night and wondered about Mel. He and Darwin had taken me on a wonderful tour of the farm late in the afternoon. It seemed we'd traveled to every far corner of it. We'd even walked to the woods at the back of his property. There was a dust-covered lane to take us there. On the way we read the powdery page that invited wildlife to mark their presence in our lives with their tracks—field mice and raccoons, and larger footprints of a dog or perhaps a red fox. The tiniest tracks of all, Mel said, were spider tracks.

Everything seemed wide open for inspection. Mel was eager to show me the barn and other buildings, so I was surprised when he stopped me abruptly as I led the way to a small outbuilding not far from the corncrib and implement shed. The door was almost obscured by a trumpet vine that seemed to have overtaken the place. By October many of the leaves were dropping, and the thing looked like a strange mythical sculpture silhouetted against the deep afternoon sun. I walked closer to inspect it, but Mel stopped mid-sentence and changed our course. "We need to get on back now. It's time for chores," he'd said. The words were innocent enough, but there was a strange tone in his voice, and his body stiffened as he grabbed my arm and pulled me from my vantage point to steer me toward the barn.

As I turned to go, I glimpsed a heavy chain that wrapped around a secure-looking latch fastened with a padlock. In these parts people don't usually lock anything, even their houses and their cars.

I lay awake for a while wondering why Mel had acted like that. The more I thought about it, the stranger it seemed. And later, as I later sipped the coffee that would help me get through another day at work, I was still wondering.

6

AT THE MEDICAL CENTER I spied Howard Ewert pacing the floor of the waiting room, looking tense and angry. "What the heck is going on here?" He kicked a lightweight chair and it fell sidewise. He didn't bother to right it and strode toward me, rudely demanding to know what was happening.

I cringed as several people looked up from magazines. I'd bumped into Kyra's father and her mother, Betty, at Kyra's apartment several times. On the whole, they seemed like decent, caring people. It hadn't been easy to accept the fact their daughter had schizophrenia and was on disability, but that was the only way she could afford the expensive medications. Otherwise Howard and Betty would have gone bankrupt trying to pay the medical bills of their young-adult daughter. Betty coped by becoming a volunteer support-group leader for family members, but Howard refused to get involved.

"Why in the name of Hades can't these people tell me if my daughter was brought into the ER? You sure as hell better tell me right now what's going on or I'll file a grievance. I'm going to get some answers. Are you taking care of her, or not?" Again, his voice was ten decibels too loud; his florid face and the nasty tone let me know he was barely containing a tide of profanity in the clenched fists at his sides.

My insides were quaking and my knees felt like Jell-O. After years of working in mental health, I could handle almost anything, but verbal abuse like that always cut me to the core. I couldn't think of what to say or do and could barely breathe. I wanted to run out the front door of the hospital and escape to anywhere.

Fortunately the hospital volunteer behind the front desk saw what was happening and came bustling to my rescue. She took a look at the Helping Hands badge hanging from the key holder around my neck. "Please come this way, Mr. Ewert. You can talk with Ms. Halstead in the consultation room down the hall."

Betty, who had been sitting in a chair in the corner pretending to read, put her magazine aside and stood up. I was relieved she was there, but I could feel her embarrassment.

I'd already discovered that the hospital hadn't permitted a parental visit after the staff identified Kyra as a Helping Hands client. "To their credit," I told the distressed parents, "they were only doing their job."

"We'll need to get a signed release form because Kyra is an adult and has the right to withhold any information she wants to from her parents. I realize these rules seem unnecessary most of the time, but they do protect people," I reassured the Ewerts.

I couldn't help thinking about the difficulties—even for Kyra—posed by well-meaning family members. Unhealthy codependency can develop in the face of necessary but over-functioning support. Parents want so badly to help. They go overboard trying to make sure their children won't be re-hospitalized—or end up homeless. I've seen it more than once. Kyra's parents kept a watchful eye on her, even though she lived apart from them. Legally, adult patients have rights, including the right to privacy about health concerns, mental or otherwise.

"I know it seems terribly unfair to you," I told

Howard and Betty. "You've spent so much time trying to help Kyra be independent, while giving her your support and encouragement. I will get this sorted out right away. You are such wonderful parents to her and this must be so hard for you." I had to admit to myself, though, that right then Howard didn't seem very wonderful.

My heart stopped pounding as I gained strength and took charge of the situation. My explanations also had a calming effect on the Ewerts. I told them I'd look in on Kyra and come back the minute I had her name on a signed release, and that they should remain there in the consulting room until I returned for them.

Kyra had been lodged in a semi-private room. She was dozing when I entered, and I noted that the staff had apparently been aware of her medications because Clozaril and a couple of other medications I recognized were listed on the chart near her bed. Kyra's face looked puffy, and she had an IV drip going. She looked confused when she opened her eyes.

"Hi, Kyra. You're in the medical center with a pretty serious leg fracture and some stitches in your arm. Are you hurting pretty bad?" I tried to be calm and soothing as I spoke quietly, yet cheerfully.

Kyra didn't lift her head off the pillow. Her speech was odd, kind of slow and deliberate. "I heard them coming and I didn't want them to take me. My refrigerator was sending electric into the picture and the glow hurts my eyes at night. You should tell Tommy to get my cat or the electric will make CAT dizzy." (I had always thought it clever that she named her yellow tiger cat CAT and pronounced it "See a tee.")

"Over on the outer edge there's a flatbed," she continued, "and we can make the dazzle brighter with sparkle. Can you put my paints under the bed and get me a bottle

63

of water? This water is poisoned." She gestured toward the blue pitcher on the hospital tray. "I want my paints. Can you get my paints?"

It was obvious to me from this word salad that Kyra was both paranoid and delusional. Yet for Howard and Betty's sake, I was pleased to see by her reference to the cat and her request for her paints that she wasn't totally out of touch with reality.

"Kyra, I'll be glad to get things taken care of for you at home just as soon as I leave here. There is something I need to ask you first though. You never signed a release form for us, and I need to know if it is okay for your parents to visit. Are you okay with having them come to see you here in the hospital?"

I purposely kept the form inside the folder I was carrying, because I didn't want to force her to do something she wasn't ready to do. It's important for powerless people to have a voice, even if it's used to refuse something like medication or parental visits. At least that's the official stance of the agency.

"That's okay," Kyra said weakly.

"I thought that is what you'd say," I told her. "They're really worried about you. In fact, I bumped into them down in the waiting room and they'd like to come up and see you right now, if that's okay." I held out the form and handed her a pen.

Her hand shook as she scrawled her name on the line beside my X.

"I'll be back this evening to check in on you. Now I'm going to take care of CAT. Do you think Tommy would feed him? I'll find your paints and bring them so you know they are safe." Tommy was her next-door neighbor, a young single man who was legally blind but could easily manage to care for the cat along with his Seeing Eye dog, Courtney.

On the way out of the medical center, I stopped briefly in the consulting room and gave the okay to Kyra's parents. Then I headed across town, sipping the last of the cold coffee in my mug as I drove.

Kyra's apartment was locked, but the building supervisor opened it for me because he was familiar with my role in Kyra's life. We stood there taking in the chaos. CAT charged toward us and I stooped to pet him. He arched his back under my hand and I felt a familiar rush of . . . something. I bent lower and continued to stroke his fur, keeping my eyes on the sleek texture and focusing on the tiny tiger stripes that wrapped around his fat middle. His eyes gleamed yellow and he looked frightened. I felt clumsy as I realized the building super was watching me. My stomach knotted and I stood up, surprised that my eyes were full of tears.

"Thanks so much for letting me in." I wiped my eyes. "I'll check in with you later on. I guess Tommy will probably take care of CAT. Your building is the only subsidized housing unit I know of that allows pets. And they're so good for people."

"Yeah, no problem," said the super as he jangled his keys.

Kyra's small living room was strewn with the remains of her artwork: broken plaster, scraps of fabric, and smashed picture frames. It looked as if a tornado had hit the room. She was a gifted artist, but not the kind who showed her work in public. I'd heard someone call her an "outsider artist," unschooled and unconnected to the established art world, but an artist all the same. The intruder had ruined every single piece of artwork in sight. Fabric pieces were slashed or torn; the remains littered the floor and the shabby end tables. I wondered if the criminal might be someone known to Kyra who was jealous of her talent.

I poked around the kitchen, looking for cat food and feeling unsettled about my tears as I stroked CAT's soft fur. I sank down on Kyra's tired once-elegant sofa and rested my elbows on my knees. An emotional tidal wave engulfed me, and two seemingly unrelated feelings came together with powerful intensity. Howard Ewert's abusive words rang in my ears as I bent down near Kyra's door and stroked CAT's soft fur. I carried her to the sofa and we sank together into the sagging cushions.

❦

Without warning I flashed back to St. John, New Brunswick, with my then-husband, Don, during dissertation days. One evening, a small tabby had shown up on the back stoop where I rested after a long day at the nursing home. I was working there while Don finished his PhD. He was gone for yet another evening and it brought comfort to entertain this scrawny, almost-grown kitten with ears too big for his head.

When Don came home late that night, the tabby was curled up beside me on the bed, and both of us were asleep. "Get that damned cat off my pillow," he'd yelled. I awakened with a start as my husband dived for the cat and almost caught her. She escaped and ran for cover under a living-room chair. He continued with a stream of abuse, and I scrambled out of bed and threw on my robe. He pushed me hard, and I fell against the door frame with such force my shoulder was wrenched and my ribs bruised. I felt it for days afterward.

Calmly I walked trancelike to the sink for a glass of water, disconnected from my true self. That was often my escape hatch—a glass of water. I smelled the beer on my husband's breath, steadied myself, and knew the shouting would continue into the wee hours of morning. I knew I should leave the house, but I felt powerless to do so.

Back then, my social-worker skills were fresh out of college. I used every technique in the book in an effort to calm my husband and reason with him. What I didn't understand until much later, too late, was that he probably had bipolar disorder. The ups and downs of our relationship left me feeling alternately elated and hopeful or full of despair. Finally, at some point, I caved in to deep sadness and understood, without being told by anyone, that I'd been utterly abandoned by the one I'd hoped would be a lifelong companion to me.

By four that morning in St. John, I had apologized to my husband and promised to take the tabby to the Humane Society—in a few days. That seemed like a compromise to me, because Don was pushing me to take her first thing in the morning. All that week I fed her and pretended I was looking for her owners while I stroked her fur. Every time I stooped to touch her in Don's presence, I felt his eyes on me, filled with utter disgust and silent hostility.

Within months our marriage ended, but not until he had almost finished his dissertation. Everything turned out wrong. When I came home from a twelve-hour shift at the nursing home to find a grad student's blond head resting on my pillow, I knew it was hopeless and time to leave.

I don't know. Maybe I packed that pain somewhere inside me when I packed up my belongings and returned to Hilldale with almost nothing, to start over.

❦

CAT purred while I cried and dabbed at my eyes, foolishly worrying about the condition of my mascara. Finally,

I returned to the task at hand, surveying Kyra's trashed apartment. Earlier in the day the police had come to investigate, but I held little hope for any forthcoming information about the assault and break-in. I was overcome by another wave of despair as I thought about how important these art projects had been in Kyra's recovery process during the past few months and how insignificant my People and their belongings seemed to be in the eyes of law enforcement. When you're poor and live in public housing, it's assumed you've invited trouble into your life—or that you've made your own trouble and deserve whatever happens to you.

The deputy had ruled out an assault by anyone living in the building. I now suspected she was a victim of a random act of violence, and the chances of finding out who committed the crime seemed slim to none. Whoever did it was a barbarian in my eyes, but probably not considered by the authorities to be worth tracking. I was filled with contempt for them as I picked up the soft fabric sculptures Kyra had been working on most recently. She'd collected odd fabric scraps and unusual buttons, which she'd glued onto fabrics culled from Goodwill's scrap pile. We'd bought her a large container of white glue, and she'd padded the sculptures with fiberfill from an old sofa cushion. The pieces took shape under her hands as she continued to add acrylic paint, buttons, thread and yarn, and then more scraps.

Some of her creations had incorporated words or letters or pictures clipped from glossy magazines. The last time I'd stopped in, she'd been adding final details to the one I liked best. She had sprinkled the entire piece with glitter and secured some sequins with more glue. I'd noticed how totally engrossed she could become in her creative work and, in truth, I envied her creative genius.

Now I stepped over the remains of that project, which had been slashed with a large kitchen knife that lay on the floor nearby. I wondered why the police hadn't take the knife as possible evidence, but it clearly didn't have any blood on it. The critical incident report said the cuts on Kyra's arm were caused by her fall against the sharp corner of the glass coffee table, the top of which lay broken in two pieces against an overstuffed chair. But I didn't move anything, just in case someone still needed to gather evidence.

I searched the bedroom jammed with clothes and two-dozen pairs of shoes, looking for Kyra's paints. Despite the clutter of her place, she always kept her art materials stacked neatly in a plastic storage box, which we had purchased for her soon after I received her case. I finally found it behind the bed, but the paints had been dumped out. I fished under the bed and came up with more supplies, which I returned to the storage box.

Before I left, I gathered a few scraps of her artwork and a couple of the damaged sculptures and placed them loosely in a grocery bag. Maybe I could save some of it for her as the art therapist might suggest doing. Maybe Kyra would be glad to have it back someday. Not today, but someday.

Tommy met me in the hallway and asked about the apartment and Kyra. I couldn't say much—client confidentiality—but talked about CAT and thanked him for helping out. I went back inside and brought him the cat food I'd found. CAT seemed willing to follow the two of us, with Tommy's dog, Courtney, leading the way down the hall.

"You know," Tommy said to me confidently. "An amazing number of gifted people had mental problems. Think about Beethoven."

"And of course Picasso and Van Gogh," I added, then suddenly remembered he had probably never seen

Guernica or *Starry Night*. "The intruder destroyed almost all her artwork," I told him.

"I know." Apparently the apartment gossip had reached him by then.

"When you see something like this you always want to find a logical reason for it," I said. "You want to blame someone. Maybe someone saw the wonderful things she did and felt jealous. Maybe it was a random act. Do you know, was there someone who was jealous of her work or who gave her trouble before this?"

"I don't know. I can't think of anyone," said Tommy. "It's just that she was so happy doing art and now she's all sick and in the hospital and everything. I wish we would have looked out for her more."

"I wish this hadn't happened," I told him. "But we can't blame ourselves. That won't help matters at all."

"This has to be hard for her to take. It would be for anyone. I have a couple of pieces of artwork I made during college. You know, a pottery bowl and a couple of water-colors, and a big charcoal sketch. I even have that one framed and hanging in my hallway. I can imagine how angry and upset I'd be if someone came in and destroyed my pictures.

"Kyra will feel terrible when she sees what they did. She will need a lot of support and understanding, and I know you and some of the others here can give that to her."

"Yeah, we can try," Tommy said. We'd been chatting in the hallway and now he opened the door and ushered CAT and Courtney into his living room.

I walked to the parking lot, still thinking about who might have hurt Kyra and trying to accept the idea that I'd probably never know much more than I knew right then.

ℰ

I finished my workday by stopping briefly to check in with a couple of my People who lived independently just beyond the city limits. It was a good feeling being back in my car, out on the country roads on a beautiful autumn day, much nicer than Saturday. The sky was especially blue and the trees were holding their colors longer this year because frost was so late in coming. I thought then about paint and color and wondered if Kyra would start painting again. Or would she be so upset about losing her work that she'd refuse to try? I promised myself I'd encourage her. She needed her art.

I thought, "If I ever paint again, I would want to paint the sky and trees the way everything looks today." But I had too much to do and was tired when a day was over. A day like that one, with a stop for a fast-food dinner and a second hospital visit, would take every bit of energy I had to get through it. I didn't even know where my art supplies were anymore. Probably packed away somewhere in Mom's attic. I had other, more important priorities.

I drove slowly down a winding country road—a shortcut I'd found. My mind wandered again to the weekend, Mel Martin, and my fall from grace in choosing to see Darwin while off duty. It seemed almost unthinkable in the light of another workday that I'd spent the weekend out there on that farm and then driven Darwin home after dark.

I resolved to put the entire thing out of my mind. But the more I tried, the harder it became. I watched as the red sun sank below the crisping cornfields. The penultimate glow of a Tuesday afternoon shimmered through the fading roadside grasses. I settled further into myself, dreaming of the dark kitchen and the peaceful quiet of Mel's home-place.

As I slowed the car to forty miles per hour, I took a deep breath and let go. I cried about the cat and everything that was connected to that one feeling. My breath shook in short little quakes, like when I was a kid and cried hard for a long time and then stopped. When you remember to breathe, you calm yourself down. After a few more deep breaths, I began thinking that change—for Darwin, for me, for anyone—is possible.

7

"RHONDA, HI! I didn't expect to see you here." Rhonda was outside the door in front of Common Grounds when I bumped into her Thursday afternoon.

"I came to town to pick up some office supplies and decided to get a couple of pounds of Equal Exchange for church before I go home. Do you have a few minutes? We could go back inside for a coffee. I haven't seen you in a while."

Whenever I met up with Rhonda, it seemed as if she had time for me. She truly cared about what was happening in my life. Fortunately, the case visits were finished early for once, so we went inside. At the counter we decided to share a large oatmeal cookie and sat breaking off bites between sips of Columbia Supremo.

"How *are* you?" Rhonda asked, looking me in the eye. I had the urge to look away rather than meet her frank gaze, but didn't.

"I don't know. I'm having a tough time right now at work. There's a lot going on and I'm having trouble keeping up. Sometimes I wonder if I'm making a difference for anyone. The problems seem never-ending, and they are compounded by poverty and a system that has so many rules. . . ." My voice trailed off as I realized there were things I couldn't—wouldn't—say to Rhonda.

She looked at me expectantly, and I didn't know what to say next.

"It has to be tough working where you do. What do

you do for fun? Are you taking care of yourself?"

"I'm doing okay, I guess. Compared to my People, I've got a pretty good life. I go to the health club and stuff. It's just that once in a while, it's hard to explain, but I almost get the feeling they have something I don't."

"Like?"

"Well, one of my People is an artist—really, she's a very good artist. I have to tell you I almost envy her all that free time to paint and make fabric sculptures and so on. Here I am working just to keep her going, maintain her independence and stay on medications, and all of that. She collects SSDI and indulges herself in creativity. Of course, I guess she couldn't work if she wanted to, because no job she could get would pay her enough to afford the medications she needs. See what I mean?"

As soon as I'd said it, I felt guilty. And silly. Imagine being jealous of one of my People. I'd never realized I felt so resentful until I heard myself say it.

"Well, doing creative work isn't a luxury, is it?" Rhonda asked, picking up on the least offensive of my comments.

"I suppose not. It's just that I'm so busy I don't have time for that stuff."

"You don't *make* time for it," Rhonda said.

"Maybe sometime later, but not right now. I've got too much going on. Some of our People are so needy. It all seems so unfair sometimes. There are days I just feel like I'm a paid friend for my People." I was embarrassed by how I was whining, but Rhonda was handling it well.

"You strike me as being a very dedicated public servant," she told me. "I know it can't be easy." Her sympathetic eyes searched my face, and I felt something like panic rising inside me.

"I am just so burned out right now," I confessed. I felt

the lump in the back of my throat and looked away to avoid giving in to the tears I felt forming behind my eyeballs.

Rhonda picked up her cup and sipped slowly, tactfully looking away. I studied the amateur painting hanging on the brick wall beside our table. Sensing I wasn't ready to reveal more, Rhonda started talking about an upcoming meeting at the Church of the Crucified Redeemer. I half listened and took in our surroundings. The battered thrift-shop tables and chairs and the thirty-year-old aqua sofa reminded me of Darwin's living room. These had been placed at Common Grounds for decorative effect. At his house it was pure function.

"I guess I'd better move on," I heard Rhonda say. "This has been nice."

"Oh, yes. Sorry. I guess I was daydreaming there, distracted by the décor in here. Pretty strange, huh?"

Rhonda nodded, and we scooped the paper remains of our fellowship into a hand-painted trashcan before parting on the sidewalk with a hug.

℮

A week later Kyra was doing much better, having spent three days in the hospital and another three in the state hospital to regulate her medication. Often a crisis leads to medication changes. The stress of her assault had caused her to decompensate. (Oh, that word again!) The mania would subside with the addition of a new antipsychotic drug, the psychiatrist had said during a case hearing at the state hospital. The medication could be used as she felt the need for it. I was glad they were encouraging her to self-monitor this way, rather than rely solely on the decision of the doctor.

It also had been decided she would stay with her parents while her leg was in the cast. This bothered me, given Howard's reaction that day in the hospital. I knew I'd be thankful when she was able to move back to her apartment in a month or so. After checking with the police to make sure they were finished with their investigation, I called a housekeeping service about cleaning up the apartment.

℃

I saved my visit to Darwin for the end of the day, partly out of habit and partly due to necessity, because he was working a four-day week now that I'd solved his transportation problem.

Darwin answered the door immediately and I realized he'd been waiting for me. He held a bulky, ceramic ashtray in one hand and a cigarette in the other. As I looked around at the odd assortment of dusty stuff in the house, I envied how much he enjoyed his things.

I could tell he had showered and shaved after returning from work. I took this as a sign of progress in his recovery, until I realized he'd put on some strong cologne or after-shave—likely Brut from a Clubhouse gift exchange—but I wondered if this touch was specifically to impress me. He wore a blue-and-white striped polo shirt that looked almost new.

I was surprised how good it felt to see him again. His thick, blond hair fell in a wild shock across his forehead, and he tossed it back with a shake of his head. I greeted him warmly with a demeanor that wasn't as artificial as my usual social-worker act.

Darwin was an unusual case for a number of reasons, not the least of which was that he was a property owner. Fortunately for him, he was able to live independently in the small house on the edge of Hilldale that his mother left him at her death. There were admittedly a few problems with the arrangement, mainly that the house was starting to need repairs to the roof and windows, and Darwin had neither the funds nor the wherewithal to see to them. I made a note to check that afternoon with the Housing Coalition or HUD to see if some grant monies had come through that could be used for repairs. Ideally, that would happen before winter.

Darwin could entertain a person for hours with his "funky junk," as I liked to think of it. I decided to listen and model the caring interest I wished he'd begin to show for others. Usually I was in a hurry, but for once I had time to look at his endless collection of fifties and sixties memorabilia and hear all about it.

He was a self-proclaimed expert on the two decades and there was a part of me that enjoyed his stuff immensely. I could browse there and be transported magically to another time and place. There was something about seeing a stack of pink and turquoise melamine dinnerware with its squarish cups and saucers that transported me instantly back to childhood. I could stand there for a long time, looking at those awful, fruit-shaped ceramic wall plaques or at the still-useful lava lamp. The scents brought back my grandmother's farm kitchen or the dusty quietness of my great-aunt's Sunday parlor, where I had sat primly on a scratchy, burgundy sofa, eating a large square of excessively sweet fruit-cocktail cake and drinking orange pop out of a small soda bottle like the one in Darwin's collection. He'd grouped his bottle collection on an enamel and white Hoosier cupboard. I instinctively knew the pull-out flour bin was full of . . . almost anything.

"Where do you get all this stuff?" I had asked Darwin on one of my first visits.

"Oh, here and there," he replied evasively.

I happened to know more than I'd let on. He was a pack rat and it was a problem. He'd been seen around town in various neighborhoods on garbage day, going through bags, presumably looking for this funky junk. He carried a dirty canvas bag with him, and some of the workers at the mental-health center were starting to keep notes and report on the frequency of his rummaging behavior. If it got too bad he could get arrested. Law enforcement had already been contacted twice by upset residents in one of the wealthier neighborhoods, but we'd spoken with them and had an understanding. They were supposed to call me right away if they had a complaint.

I had tried to figure out how to encourage Darwin's interests without causing more rummaging. I'd talked to him about it early on, and he had seemed to understand that he was exhibiting inappropriate behavior, yet I knew he persisted in his collecting. He'd simply gotten more discreet, even secretive. I'd tried to encourage him to go to flea markets, auctions, and antique malls to satisfy his desire for collecting. I'd even taken him myself once or twice. I'd also been urging him to continue organizing and displaying his stuff, although I didn't want to overdo *that* or his obsessive-compulsive tendencies might get out of control again.

The job at Farnswalters was helping redirect his energy into more positive activities. I was happy to see that there hadn't been as much garbage-collecting. The meds might also have been helping. We're never completely sure what contributes to positive outcomes. At any rate, Darwin had spent more time that summer working in his yard and small garden. He'd planted flowers, several tomato plants, and a zucchini plant that had almost overtaken the small garden plot. He was constantly giving me zucchini.

I commented on the change I saw in the way his collections were being organized. That may have been a mistake, because the next thing I knew I was confronted with an extremely talkative Darwin, who forced a thick slice of zucchini bread on me, served on a deep-purple melamine plate, of course. He led me into his small dining room, which was more of a nook than a room. There he proceeded to pull open the middle drawer of a very large, 1940s-era buffet.

An hour later, I felt as if I'd been taken on a virtual tour of Vietnam—albeit a personal and emotional one. I may have been the first guest to ever glimpse Darwin's vast collection of letters and photographs from the era. Each letter was carefully preserved in its own sheet protector. Notebooks were covered with pictures from news magazines. He'd glued collages of soldiers' photos onto the front of discarded business manuals, apparently salvaged from the dumpster of one of the local manufacturing companies. A heavy coat of white glue provided a permanent glaze on the covers. I'd almost forgotten there was such a thing as decoupage, but Darwin had used it to great advantage on his scrapbook covers.

He opened one to a letter. "Dear Love," it began.

How are you? I'm fine. I'm sorry it took me so long to write. I've been busy flying combat missions and we leave early in the morning and come back late at night. The sights and sounds on the ground are so disgusting I would never want to tell you about them. Let's just say—wounded civilians, little dirty kids with blood-caked faces and people with bare feet and so many injuries you know they're never going to survive no matter how you try to help. I carry the handkerchief you gave me in my pocket and just touching it gives me the strength to keep going. Do you have plans for

Christmas? I hope to stay in the air after the new year. Our unit is being transferred and they tell us we'll be flying missions over Laos. Stay as sweet as you are.

Love,
Pete

I felt a knot form in the pit of my stomach, and something lurched through my body like one of the infamous 1940s-era electroshock treatments I'd heard my aging People talk about. Darwin didn't seem to notice. I turned the page and studied a gray, stained handkerchief with frayed lace edging. It was displayed on a piece of bright-red card stock.

"Is this the one from the letter?" I whispered to Darwin, breaking the intense silence of the afternoon.

"I don't know. . . . It might be. I found it in the same garbage can over on Evergreen Street when an old couple moved out to go to the retirement home.

"I should have gone to Vietnam. Everyone else did. I had to stay home."

I looked at Darwin, slumped dejectedly in the armchair that was almost too small to hold his six-foot frame. The energy so evident at the beginning of our visit was drained from him now.

I didn't know what to say. I'd never thought about the fact that he may have been old enough to be a Vietnam vet, but I supposed it was possible if he'd been drafted near the end of the war. At any rate, seeing those scrapbooks, I knew that the war was, in many ways, as painful for him as if he'd actually served. He had collected all those letters and other mementos and so carefully arranged them and compiled them into a poignant, personal, and private collection of pain, as if it could in some way absolve him of the guilt he felt about not fighting with his peers in Vietnam. He'd probably been deferred because of his mental illness—just one more guilt-inducing consequence of having a brain disorder during those formative years of young adulthood, a consequence never recognized by me or the dozens of other professionals who'd tried to help him through the years.

I sat silently looking at Darwin. Unbidden, tears flooded my eyes. He took the scrapbook gently from my hands and closed it carefully and slowly, smoothing the page with his fingertips. (Later I thought about it and was surprised at this gesture of care for me.) I stared at the dust-coated fiberglas drapes, unseeing, feeling blank and empty-headed. My heart ached for all the pain in the world, and for Darwin, who carried some deep and, until now, unrecognized scar that I had probably only glimpsed briefly in those moments.

I rummaged in my bag for a tissue while Darwin shifted uncomfortably in his chair. Then he reached across the table to pick up the plate with its half-eaten green-flecked offering. As he moved toward me, he suddenly stopped midway and reached awkwardly to squeeze the back of my hand where it rested palm down on the plastic lace table-cloth. I felt the warmth of his calloused palm and didn't pull away.

Darwin's eyes met mine, and I felt weak and unsure of where to look or what to say. Vietnam was such a long time ago. Some of us go for weeks never giving it a thought. I recognized that there are others who never live an hour without thinking about it. And this is true not only for those who went, but also for some of those who did not go. The Vietnam legacy is not only the history of soldiers who fought there and survived, or of families who received their loved one home in a body bag. Everything, and every person alive then was affected by it. Is it healthy to preserve those memories and collect our pain into scrapbooks? I didn't know. But I had more respect for Darwin and better understood what might have shaped his outlook.

At the door, Darwin reached again for my hand and I pulled away self-consciously, wishing I could bridge the prohibition against physical contact. A hug would have been comforting to both of us right then, but our roles dictated otherwise. Without thinking I said, "Darwin, I care about you so much." The tears were still brimming in my eyes. "Please take care of yourself . . . because I love you."

I turned and walked down the sidewalk to my car. As I got in and fastened my seat belt, I glanced toward the house and saw Darwin standing there lighting a cigarette and watching me through the window of the storm door.

8

I WAS TOO FAMILIAR with the bone-weary tiredness that settled over me most days as soon as I arrived home. I entered the door and fell onto the sofa, wondering where I would find the energy to microwave a Lite Gourmet Entrée and open the bag of instant salad that had become my habitual dinner.

The scene at Darwin's house was still troubling me. I kicked off my shoes and waited for the kettle whistle. The exhaustion didn't lead to conscious thoughts so much as to a tightness in my shoulders and an ache across my back. I walked on the knots that had swelled on the soles of my feet. The tension moved silently through my extremities and settled into the muscles of my neck until I felt knotted pain instead of weariness.

It wasn't Darwin exactly, but the whole mix of feelings that had been brewing for the last while. Feelings of dissatisfaction and anger like those I'd described to Rhonda in the coffee shop. And there was another vague, unsettled, lost feeling. Darwin had stirred up something inside me and, just as the outburst of Howard Ewert had led to personal grief, I had a momentary suspicion this latest tearful incident with Darwin might too.

I don't cry easily, but it had happened twice in the space of two days. What was that violent feeling of unrest I'd had as we looked at his scrapbooks? And then that almost uncontrollable urge to hug him. Oh, no! What had I done? I'd told him I loved him! It scared me, because it betrayed a neediness I'd been ignoring for far too long.

The time had already changed over to daylight savings time, and through the window I watched the sky getting darker. I dreaded the long, dark evenings and reminded myself to enjoy solitude, as Rhonda had been teaching me. I picked up one of my favorite books, not to read, but to nibble on some inspiration that I hoped would get me through the next hour or two. I needed a distraction, but nothing interested me.

I thought of calling Rhonda, but what would I say to her? "Hello, Rhonda? This is Angie. I'm trying to do solitude, but it's coming off as lonely. Any suggestions?" Rhonda may have been a good friend, but doing something like that was out of the question. I'd have to tough it out by myself.

Maybe tomorrow night when Sister Source met for a special presentation on "The Kairos Document: Challenge to the Church"—maybe we'd talk then. The group had decided to explore that theological comment on the 1980s political crisis in South Africa to help us look at the concept of justice and reconciliation. I liked the way Rhonda was concerned about social issues. She was always stretching her church members at the Crucified Redeemer to move beyond prevalent religious thought. She talked about restorative justice.

I liked Rhonda, and I liked her best as a person who was there for me, someone to talk to about my personal life—the spirituality thing. When she got into her social justice stuff she annoyed me sometimes. Maybe I'd heard too much of that growing up. But anyway, the meeting would give me something else to think about besides this confusing stuff with Darwin.

In its recyclable plastic dish, the chicken almandine with rice pilaf had been reduced to a pool of sauce that didn't lend itself to being eaten with a fork. I was contemplating a bubble bath when the phone rang.

"Hello."

"Hello, Angie. This is Mel Martin. How are you?"

I was surprised to hear his voice, and given the mental state I was in, a strange feeling of unreality suddenly overtook me. For a split second it was as if I were someone else, getting a call from a person I didn't know. I pushed the almandine away from me on the coffee table and, out of habit, grabbed a notepad (Family Center for Behavioral Health, Gravenburg).

"Fine," I said, then, after his pause, "Well, yeah, I'm okay, I guess." I knew I sounded as tentative as I felt about my condition at that moment. "How about you?"

There was more silence, and I felt compelled to fill it. "I was just thinking about you. I saw Darwin today. He's doing pretty well."

I hadn't been thinking about Mel, but it seemed fortuitous that Darwin's uncle called on the very evening I was obsessing about the late-afternoon case visit at Darwin's place. "Yeah, he actually served me a piece of zucchini bread he baked from the crop in that garden of his."

Mel laughed heartily. "I suppose he served it on some of his prized melamine dinnerware."

"Exactly."

"I've been thinking I should call and find out more about those classes for families that you mentioned. I've been having Darwin come down here to help me from time to time, and I thought I could learn more about his problems. When are they starting a new one?"

"I wish I could tell you, Mel. I don't have the date here at home." I was surprised Mel was calling me at home anyway, because the only thing I'd given him was my card with an office number. I supposed I wasn't that hard to find in the phone book; I didn't have an unlisted number like a lot of case managers.

"What are you doing these days besides eating zucchini bread with Darwin?" Mel asked. There was a sardonic tone in his voice that suggested familiarity.

"Not much. Watching it get dark and wondering how I'm going to get through the winter. How about you?"

"Oh, I guess I live in the dark most of the time," Mel said. "But we don't complain about the weather like you do in the city. We figure whatever we got coming we can handle. 'It rains on the just and the unjust,' as they say. Why fight it?"

"Yeah, I suppose that makes sense."

"Really, for farmers, winter is kind of nice. Not as much work to do, plenty of time for reading. That's why I was thinking of taking the class now, if it's offered. Just let me know. I can call tomorrow night, if that's okay."

"I'll be out tomorrow night. Why don't you call me the night after. I'll bring the flyer home with me. I think you'll really like the class. Some of the families that have taken it are so enthusiastic about it. The customer satisfaction surveys the agency's gathered show that the classes contribute positively to the consumer's recovery process. Making information about psychiatric conditions accessible to the family member is contributing to positive outcomes for many of our clients. I'm sure you'd find it helpful."

Suddenly, I hated how quickly I'd slipped into my social worker language. I just wanted to be a regular woman talking to a guy on the phone. I wanted to ask Mel about his dog and find out what kinds of things he was doing on the farm. His comment about reading flitted through my head and I thought about all his books and notebooks. Farmers must have to understand a lot more technical things than I realized, but Mel didn't talk in jargon, so why did I? I pictured us on the brief farm tour and for a split second had a vision of the mysterious padlocked door.

"How's your dog?"

"Oh, Buster? He's great. Starting to grow his winter coat. I almost took him along to town with me this evening, but then decided to eat dinner at the Café del Rio, so he stayed home."

It is a wonder—the names people give to restaurants in those small, out-of-the-way places. You'd think they would call it something like Harvest Home Diner, which would fit so much better with the geography. But no, Café del Rio it is, if you live down south of Hilldale. Maybe, on second thought, it's their way of getting some variety into an otherwise ordinary existence. "Yup, honey, I'm goin' down to Café' del Rio for some burritos and refried beans. Wanna come along?" After all, if it's chicken and noodles you want, you can get that at home. Idly I wondered if Mel ever ate Lite Gourmet.

"Well, I gotta go. No use running up a bill here. I'll call you about seven on Thursday. Talk to you later. Bye."

"Yeah, bye, Mel."

I sat with the phone cradled under my chin for a second or two until I heard the dial tone. Mel had rural ways, all right, so frugal, thinking about the cost of a short phone call.

A few lines from a Seamus Heaney poem floated to my mind's surface as a reminder of the dearth of human companionship in my life. "When you have nothing more to say . . . the land without marks so you will not arrive . . . but pass through . . ."

November, I decided as I prepared myself for it, is one of those times you do pass through, just as I'd passed through that weekend on Mel's farm. I sat there thinking and promised myself I wouldn't complain about the weather to anyone and that I'd be as kind to myself as I was to others.

᷁℃

The following day I spent some extra time with Kyra, taking her to several appointments, including one for an X-ray to see how her bone was healing. She was wearing bright pink canvas shoes and a long skirt made of several different fabrics. The oversized velveteen bag went everywhere with her.

She seemed to be on the way to recovery—at least from the broken bone. There was nothing to do but wait for the cast to come off in a few weeks. She was back on her regular medication schedule with an extra prescription for Haldol, in case her voices got too bad. Living with her family seemed to be going well. I thought about healing and wished the psychiatric condition could heal as easily as a broken bone.

"I was wondering, Angie," she said. She spoke with that soft, inflection-free voice I associated with pronounced flat affect.

"Yes, Kyra, what were you wondering?" I smiled encouragingly at her. She was so hesitant to ask for favors.

"Could we stop by the bank? I could get some cash and then maybe go to the art store before we go home. I want some new pastels."

"What a great idea!" I said a bit too enthusiastically. I find myself wishing for some enthusiasm in our talk, but it always comes from me, making our stilted conversations even more unbalanced.

"The Clubhouse got big end-rolls of newsprint, and they told me to take one home."

Many of our People on disability attended programs at the Clubhouse, where they enjoyed a certain comfort in being able to socialize with friends who've had similar experiences. The art and writing classes were especially popular.

"That's just wonderful, Kyra. Do you have a place to work?"

"My brother came over and fixed up an easel for me using some scrap lumber he had. Have you seen the sky lately?" The abrupt change of subject wasn't a surprise, and I confessed that I hadn't been paying much attention to the sky. Still, just then as I looked, I saw what she meant.

After an overcast October, we'd had a late Indian summer. Ordinarily, we'd be looking for our first snow of the year. Yet all signs pointed to an extended time of unseasonably good weather still ahead.

The trees kept their color longer than usual that October, but only a few oaks still had their leaves, which would hold on all winter. This time of year, the land, the hills, and the valleys on the edge of the Allegheny plateau take on the stark, quiet serenity of a barren wilderness, though we know the brown, dry season is only temporary.

With her quiet observation, Kyra had opened my eyes. I watched the sky the rest of that week and the next, wondering what she would produce on her newsprint with the pastels.

I thought of buying a box of pastels for myself but didn't give in to the impulse. As I drove home each evening and down country roads during the afternoon, I watched the sky and wondered if I'd ever really seen it in November before. The clouds were layered with color—pink and azure and periwinkle—and the sinking sun spun in an arc through them as the horizon rose and fell across the hills. I noticed how the dome of sky cupped down against the bare fields, the dormant pastures, and the newly visible woodlands.

I drove home the long way, through a rural township southeast of Hilldale, not caring if I got lost. The red barns, white houses, and long lanes with mailboxes at the end looked clean and strong against the bare landscape. I thought about how beautiful November can be. Why hadn't I ever noticed before?

9

WHEN I WALKED into the Church of the Crucified Redeemer that evening, the scent of strong coffee greeted me at about the same moment Rhonda hurried to my side with a handsome African-American man, Dr. Gavin Larch. She was eager to introduce us, and told me with a tone of awe in her voice that he was a visiting professor from Great Britain, teaching at Harvard Divinity School this year.

Rhonda looked excited. She was wearing one of the long denim jumpers she favored, with a white, eyelet-collared blouse. We all three made our way to the table where coffee was waiting, and I took my mug from the rack. Rhonda didn't like Styrofoam cups, and it was her idea to have pottery mugs made for us. Regulars even had their names glazed on. Seeing my own name there among the others—all of us hanging together there on the rack—gave me a feeling of belonging.

"Dr. Larch," Rhonda said, "we'd be honored if you'd accept a cup of our fairly traded brew." I prepared myself for Rhonda's enthusiastic promotion of the coffee she drank in support of the Central American farmers. She'd become a convert when she went on a "service learning tour." In Costa Rica she'd met some families whose livelihood and welfare depended on their crops of shade-grown organic coffee.

"You can almost taste the justice when you drink it," I quipped.

"And remember, when spring comes, the birds that nest in Ohio may well have wintered on a coffee farm somewhere to the south of us."

"All the more reason to pay extra for organic," I replied.

Dr. Larch listened to us with amusement. He'd be making a presentation at the local liberal arts college the following day. By offering to drive him to and from the airport, Rhonda had managed to persuade him to meet with our group. She had a habit of scheming to find ways of enlightening us about her pet topics. Tonight was a prime example.

The professor began talking to me about social work, so I assumed Rhonda had already told him about me. He listened attentively as I outlined the general duties of a case manager for people with psychiatric disabilities. His dark eyes met mine with genuine interest. "What are your challenges in the arena of social justice issues in *that* community of apartheid?" he asked expressively.

I suddenly felt out of my league and a long way from the academic community where I suspected Dr. Larch spent most of his time. "Well, I don't really know. . . . I never thought of my People as victims of apartheid, but you might have a point. I guess I'll wait to hear what you have to say before I answer that one."

It was an easy out on my part and ended our conversation just in time. Rhonda had taken her place behind the flimsy podium at the front of the room and was trying to call the group to order.

"Let's just pull our chairs into a circle," she directed. "I'm sure Dr. Larch would like that arrangement, and we may all feel more comfortable."

After we were settled I looked around the room and smiled a hello to my friends. Rhonda's husband, Dale, had been able to get off work at the car dealership, and a couple of women had brought husbands or friends, so our group was larger than the usual eight women.

I had to admit that I didn't know much about South Africa and the work of the church there in the struggle for justice. I was more informed about the injustices of Hilldale. I guess injustice is everywhere—nearby or far away. I was already thinking about how apartheid might be evidenced in Hilldale's population of "severely mentally disabled" adults, as my supervisor Barbara Delaney sometimes referred to them.

Dr. Larch handed out copies of the *Kairos Document*, a brief, six-chapter pamphlet that was the basis of a challenge set forth by South African church leaders in 1985. He explained how the development, study, and eventual implementation of the document had led to massive political change and stands as an illustration of the power of faith to shape the political climate of a country.

The word *kairos*, he told our group, is a Greek word used in the Bible to designate a special moment when God visits a people to give them a unique opportunity for change and decisive action. It is a time of judgment, a moment of truth, a crisis. It is a moment of grace and opportunity. It is different from our own understanding of linear time, which in Greek is *kronos*.

"In the 1980s," Dr. Larch began, "South African church leaders examined the prevailing theology, including the theology of many Christian churches across the globe that condoned or even supported governmental action in opposition to the basic teachings of the New Testament.

"The *Kairos Document* called for participation in the struggle for liberation and a just society. It said that over and above its regular activities, the church would need to have special programs, projects, and campaigns, not as a duplication of a secular campaign, but in partnership and solidarity with those who share the same goals."

Dr. Larch seemed a modern prophet as he spoke. His eyes flashed and his face was alive with the passion of his belief in the truth of his words. His mellow British enunciation flowed like music in the humble, storefront church. As he caught us all up in the story, it wasn't hard to imagine being in a small meeting room anywhere in the world, where people of faith might come together on behalf of those suffering oppression.

"The South African *Kairos Document* identifies the most common weakness of what many churches offer: cheap reconciliation without truth or justice. Churches want to stay away from political action. From what they think is neutrality, they attempt to issue balanced statements, in order not to fall out with any side. Or they remain silent if there appears to be the risk of potential conflict with those in power. Solidarity with victims is mostly words with no active involvement."

I thought of the Quakers who hid slaves in their barns and the Mennonite conscientious objectors who worked in the mental hospitals during World War II. They brought about big changes in the way people like Darwin and Kyra received treatment. And I thought about my own mother, who dared to speak for what she believed, and how she continued to touch so many lives as she traveled the globe assisting medical teams. I wanted to remind him of those few examples. And examples are few, I guess. The conscientious objectors who worked in the mental hospitals numbered no more than a few thousand.

Dr. Larch's voice faded in and out as my mind wandered and I thought about the kind of apartheid my People experience every day. They're forced to live in low-quality housing on government incomes that barely support them. The medicine they need can't be bought for any wages they are able to earn. Insurance policies cover medication for diabetes and heart disease, but impose severe limits for mental-health treatment and hospitalization. Options for treatment facilities are limited to one or two and are often miles from where a person lives. For my People, discrimination is part of life. For instance, theirs is the only medical condition that's fair game for use as a plot line in a murder mystery.

"I need to close now, and we will have a time for questions." Dr. Larch brought me back to the present in time to hear a generous quote from the original *Kairos Document*, which had been rewritten by several groups in other countries after it appeared in South Africa: "The church should challenge, inspire, and motivate people. It has a message of the cross that inspires us to make sacrifices for justice and liberation. It challenges us to act with hope and confidence. The church must preach this message not only in words and sermons and statements, but also through its actions, programs, campaigns, and divine services."

The room grew quiet as we sat for a moment taking in those profound yet troubling words.

Dale Kinder broke the silence with a question. "But doesn't the church in North America speak out on important social issues? It seems like there are plenty of voices speaking out—against abortion and pornography, for instance."

"True," Dr. Larch said, nodding. "But consider: Are these not perhaps the *safe* topics that sidetrack us and engage Christians in unending debate and media drama. They could in fact tarnish our image as credible thinkers and problem solvers.

"Don't misunderstand. I'm not saying these aren't legitimate issues, just that the more pressing topics are often left out of conversations about faith and social issues. Perhaps the topics we don't talk about are more politically charged and would require us to take a stand that would challenge our capitalist empire."

"I see what you mean," Dale answered. "So, looking at our society from your European vantage point, what topics should we be concerned about?"

I sensed a bit of tension in his tone, likely the result of Dr. Larch's reference to "capitalist empire." I happened to know Dale wasn't as left leaning as Rhonda. After all, he made a living selling SUVs.

"Well, for example, the churches say yes to sustainable, farm-based agriculture, but do not say no to agribusiness. Without the no being clearly defined, resistance cannot grow, the structural change will move forward while our yes is rendered ineffective."

"And, they say yes to welfare reform and rights for the disabled," I thought, "but no to equal insurance coverage for psychiatric disorders."

Our speaker continued his explanations. "The voices of nature and those of future generations are particularly easy to push aside. They are not, or not yet, able to organize themselves. Their voices are being reinforced particularly by women who suffer disadvantage or violence. Everywhere in the world women are developing new visions of life and living together."

He certainly struck a chord with our group when he mentioned the contribution of women. I looked around the circle at my Sister Source friends and saw Rhonda looking smug as she cradled her mug of coffee. She was justified in her pride in the little network of women who had formed to study and learn together.

"Women are less competitive and more community-minded sometimes, aren't they?" Rhonda asked. I sensed she was phrasing it in a way that wouldn't alienate the four men who were with us.

"Women often look not for competition but co-operation," Dr. Larch replied, "not for their own career but for community; not for profit but for relationships; not for successful conquests but for healing. Their actions belie the myth spread by economic interest groups that to provide for social needs and to have ecological aims are not compatible."

My friends were nodding in agreement.

"Such new visions are helping to overcome the spirit of complacency and to mobilize resistance against practices that diminish a full life. In many parts of the world it is the women who are getting together and working to develop new ways of living that are cooperative and ecologically sound."

Rhonda looked around the room, letting her eyes rest on each person in attendance before moving on to the next. Maybe she was taking a head count. But I knew she'd gotten what she wanted from this meeting with Dr. Larch, even if it was a gathering of just a few. I was happy for her. She was truly a gift to all of us and deserved to have that moment of triumph.

"You know," she said in response to Dr. Larch's comment about women's contributions, "in Latin America there are, for example, Pentecostal groups that cooperate with Christian communities inspired by liberation theology to achieve real improvements in people's lives. Jesus struggled against the Romans and conformist Jews for justice and peace. At the same time he lifted up women and healed people and established groups committed to mutual support and service."

"That is so true!" Dr. Larch said. "We don't have to settle for an outdated or irrelevant faith. It's all a matter of what we choose to do and where we put our energy. To what effort will you lend your voice?"

After the meeting, we walked out onto the sidewalk in

a group, with the music of Dr. Larch's voice for justice still ringing in our ears. His gentle challenge clung to us like the crisp night air. The sidewalk seemed to shine under the streetlight, and I tilted my head as Rhonda pointed out the bright appearance of Venus. Then everyone dispersed to their cars or took off quickly on foot down the sidewalk.

Just before I got in my car, I looked up at the sky once more. At that exact moment a shooting star fell across the sky just ahead of me. It spoke to me of hope for things as yet unseen—new life taking shape in the world, and also within me.

10

THE FOLLOWING EVENING I picked up a baked potato with toppings at a drive-through, and all of a sudden, as I was putting up the window, I remembered. Mel was going to call me. I hurried back to the office for the flyer of the class schedule, which was buried under a pile in my in-box.

I finally got back to my dark house with a cold supper and considered lighting the gas logs in the fireplace, just for some atmosphere.

"Does my evening in any way resemble the evenings of my People?" I wondered. They don't have gas fireplaces, but otherwise I can't generalize. Darwin might be eating a homemade zucchini casserole or an end-of-the garden stew. Kyra might be sitting at her easel. Tommy and others in the apartment building might be meeting for a potluck. I suspected some of my People felt lonely that evening but many were probably less lonely than I was.

Community seems beyond my reach so often, but there are sometimes moments of connection, like the gathering of spirits I felt after the meeting with Dr. Larch. I let my mind rest on that brief moment we'd shared in the parking lot.

For some reason, my next thought, accompanied by a feeling of impending disaster, was about the way I'd said, "I love you," to Darwin. It was so inappropriate. I'd crossed a boundary, and that could be his undoing. Or mine. I hoped he'd forget it, or that maybe he hadn't heard it.

Darwin's scrapbooks still haunted me. The tears, the

lump in the throat, the physical jolt I'd felt at seeing what he'd done. It was so uncharacteristic of me to lose control like that. "The Vietnam thing gets to me," I admitted to myself. "Maybe some old issues of mine.

"Get a grip, Angie. Get a grip." I put my potato in the microwave.

We had to maintain our roles, Darwin—the consumer —and me—the professional. I don't like that word *consumer,* used so routinely in the system. Being a consumer implies one has some choice in the matter. But Darwin had none. There was only one Helping Hands where a person like him with a disability might get assistance. That place was a community in its own right, I suppose. But my community was found elsewhere.

Thinking about it just then, I had to concede that my People might have more interdependence with their peers than I did with my mine—what with apartment-house potlucks and bridge tournaments.

The phone rang. I grabbed the cordless and ran to remove the teakettle before I answered.

"Angie, this is Mel. How are you?" There was an unpretentious quality to his voice, and he accented the word *are* in a way that sounded like he wanted to know.

"I'm enjoying the solitude," I told him as I rummaged for the flyer.

He liked my answer. "Ah, the lonely place in our lives. We should spend more time there."

That soothed me somehow. An image of the vine-covered outbuilding floated unbidden across my mind's screen saver. "Oh, *you're* never lonely, are you?" I asked lightheartedly. "Besides, I make a distinction between solitude and loneliness. Solitude is wholesome—"

"And maybe loneliness isn't?" Mel interjected.

In my mind I pictured the farm high on the hill. I

imagined the dark kitchen, the cozy room where I'd stayed, the ancient furnishings, the meal he cooked, the wonderful tour of his place, and the feeling of the wind in my hair as we walked across his fields that day. A thought was forming, but then Mel spoke.

"Angie, I keep thinking I need to apologize to you."

"How so?"

"Well, truth be told, I asked about the classes because I just felt so terrible about the way I talked to Darwin the other week when you were here. I can't get that off my mind. I shouldn't have yelled at him that way. I already apologized to him. I know that put you in an uncomfortable spot too. I'm so sorry. Can you forgive me?"

I was surprised at this confession. I'd all but forgotten the incident, but it was true that it didn't seem right when it happened. It had made me wonder about Mel.

"'A soft answer turneth away wrath.' I know better." Mel's voice softened as he quoted the proverb in King James English.

"That's all right. Sure, I'll forgive you. Now let's be friends."

My comment hung between us on the telephone wire.

"I've got the information you wanted here." I started in, business-like again. "Classes start next week. Your timing is perfect, and I do think it will help you a lot. Family members teach them, and we hold them in churches and public buildings, not at the agency. That way everyone feels comfortable with the setting. Do you know where the Church of the Crucified Redeemer is?"

"Oh, sure. Rhonda's place?"

"Exactly. Class starts at seven p.m. Will that work?"

I gave Mel the name of the group leader, Betty Ewert, Kyra's mother, who I knew would be a capable teacher for the family-support classes.

By the time we'd hung up, my potato had to be microwaved again. But I'd heard about harvesting corn. Only a few acres left, Mel had said. And how he'd have more time for tinkering once it was done. I'd have been happy to hear more if he'd wanted to share it. I was starting to like Mel, in spite of his reticence on the phone.

I wasn't even finished eating when the phone rang again.

"Angie, sorry to bother you twice in the same evening. I got ahold of Betty Ewert and there's still room in the class, so I'm signed up. I was wondering . . . when I come up next Tuesday, would you, 'um, want to have dinner beforehand?"

His question caught me off guard.

"I wouldn't want to interrupt that precious solitude you value so much," he said.

"But if it's loneliness, *that* I can take care of."

"I've had plenty of solitude and I could use a good dinner," I said, eyeing the remains of the potato.

"Me too. Where shall we go? The Tavern in Zoar?"

"Perfect!" The Tavern was one of my favorite spots, but I didn't get there often. The chef was very much the culinary artist, and his signature "Davey sauce," with its garlicky brown juices, never failed to please. It might not reflect the cuisine of the Germans who settled this Ohio village, but it was certainly popular with the Tavern's modern-day guests.

I gave Mel directions to my house. We decided to catch the early-bird special. And there it was again. Mel's frugal side. But the Tavern is pricey and he *did* have to make it to his first class by seven o'clock.

"Don't get too dressed up," Mel warned. "I'll have to bring the Dakota. The Mustang's already tucked in for winter."

℮

Balmy weather invited people out while they still had the chance. Everywhere they were exulting in the unseasonable warmth as they rode bicycles, roller-bladed through the park, or sat out on street-side patios in light-weight jackets eating one more ice cream cone. It seemed everyone was savoring the last days of Indian Summer.

I felt elated—like a high school girl—as I pulled on a new sweater and my favorite jeans for my "date" with Mel. In my world, dates weren't ever talked about, even thought about. Sometimes a few of us meet for dinner after work. I'd gone to a concert with a man from another county whom I'd met at a workshop in Columbus, but we'd just arranged to meet in the lobby of the hotel.

I was drying my hair when suddenly sparks flew from my hair dryer; I dropped it in the sink and quickly unplugged it. A loud, surprising belly laugh emerged over my silly excitement—such a hot date that I had burned up my hair dryer getting ready!

In the movies we all watch, an evening like this might end up at my place, with Mel in my bed. In the morning we'd get up and cook breakfast. Or one of us would sneak out of bed and appear wrapped in a bath towel. Soon he'd hurry out the front door with a shirttail hanging out of his trousers.

It was tantalizing to imagine Mel cooking me breakfast in my kitchen. But in real-life Hilldale, it just *ain't* gonna happen, no matter how well things go. I'm not that kind of girl, either. I've sometimes wondered why I'm such an anomaly, but maybe real life isn't as much like the movies as I think. I've been burned once too often. No, this was just for fun, for a good dinner. The Tavern in the historic German-heritage village was the perfect setting. I'd always felt at home at the tables flanked by high-backed wooden benches with their red plaid seat cushions. The bar was made from highly polished oak plank, presumably cut from one of the trees in the virgin forest that once covered this territory. It was worn to a sheen and strewn with peanut shells. Antique posters and kitchenware decorated the walls.

Mel arrived a little early. He was wearing a sweater that was probably a decade old but of high quality. I'd rarely seen him without a farm cap, and I noted his thinning blond hair behind the forelock of wheat straw. My assessment led me to conclude he was the right age for conversations about the sixties and seventies.

The sixties was always good discussion material for someone of my generation, though we were likely to talk mostly about music and clothing. We might venture into the scene on college campuses, or escapades like Woodstock. Once a guy told me how he'd packed up his belongings and left the campus after the Kent State shootings. He enrolled in a liberal arts college and never looked back. Went on to seminary, actually.

I needn't have worried about our conversation. The prescribed script of small talk started on the seat of Mel's pickup and continued until well after the hostess had seated us and the wait staff had taken our order. I studied the wine menu but thought better of it when I remembered Mel was a Mennonite and might not drink. He ordered coffee right off, not waiting for dessert, as I probably would have.

I asked Mel about his youth. His answer took a long time. He hadn't gone to college but went to Southeast Asia before it was on the evening news every night. He'd never been a particularly good student. His favorite courses in high school were shop and biology, although he also learned to like literature because of Mr. Chris, a teacher he'd had as a junior.

Back then, there wasn't a lot of career counseling. Usually the principal would call you in and go over your test scores with you. Mel's told him he "wasn't college material." But that was something he'd already figured out, he told me, so he had to think of other options. He made up his mind he was leaving the farm. He was tired of doing chores twice a day and milking cows.

Mel had grown up in a deeply religious home. His family went to church "every time the church door opened," he said. "Mennonites are one of several historic peace churches, along with Quakers." (I didn't bother to tell him, but I knew that, of course.) Mel told me how, when he was young, Mennonite men were encouraged to register with the draft board as conscientious objectors. But Mel said he had a lot of questions about that as the time drew near.

"I felt I needed to serve my country. After all, this is a great land," he said, glancing toward the shuttered window of the Tavern. It was as if he were looking for the fields just beyond Zoar. I nodded in agreement and noticed his abnormally tight jaw muscles and a crease just below his hairline. It signaled to me that, all these years later, he still felt conflict between his own beliefs and those of his family.

"That must have been hard," I commented. "How did you deal with it? What did you do?"

"Well, as it turned out," he said, "I did my own service in a way that has given me some perspectives on things most guys of my times never had."

I thought of Darwin and his Vietnam scrapbooks and wondered if Mel knew about them. I wished I could bring up the subject, but of course I couldn't risk breaching trust over what would be considered personal information regarding Darwin—although we both knew him well.

"What did you do?" I asked.

"Joined the Peace Corps and spent three years in Laos."

"That must have been quite an experience. What did you do there?"

"I worked in community development, and during the last year I was there they got me started designing appropriate technology."

"What in the heck is appropriate technology?" I asked.

"Have you ever heard of beating swords into plowshares?"

"Well, yes, but I don't get it. Were you building plows?"

"Something like that. . . ." Mel's voice trailed off as the hostess came and asked if we needed more rolls or coffee refills. When she'd left, we went back to eating our beef kabobs. I listened while Mel told his story between bites.

"I went to Laos and was there early on. I was really young, just out of high school, but I'd grown up on the farm—that farm I live on now.

"Well, I had plenty of experience with crops, dirt, manure, that sort of thing. So they put me in this tiny village out in the Xieng Khouang province. They farm there— what we'd call sustainable agriculture here—but they grow rice, not corn and oats. It's a very simple life. They live in bamboo houses with thatched roofs, and they keep a few animals, catch fish from the river, and grow rice. As community developers, we tried to improve their farming methods and introduce new breeding stock to upgrade their livestock. I worked with one other guy, and the two of us were miles from any other Americans. It was really a different world."

His story unfolded in a way that was personal, although the things he described were completely foreign to me. His voice carried me along like the waving tops of the rice seedlings he was talking about. I was transplanted to another world. It was a green world of beauty and gentleness.

As I listened to the energetic cadence of his speech, my mind wandered just a bit. I thought of *Leaves of Grass* and could picture where the book was resting on the shelf in his front room, as he would call it. I caught the strength and even a cadence of Whitman in the voice of the man across the table. His descriptions were sensuous and earthy —so earthy I could almost smell the rice paddies and hear the wind in the thatch of that other homeplace.

For once, I lost my social-worker consciousness that decreed I was always the helper and every person around me the helpee. I didn't use the mechanical active-listening skills that were now so ingrained they'd become a tired habit. I didn't watch myself respond with body language that mirrored my conversational partner across the table, thus making us both more comfortable—or self-conscious, as the case may be. I didn't work to establish the exact ratio of eye contact to no eye contact.

I fussed with the napkin on my lap and stirred my iced tea with the straw, swirling the lemon around and around in the glass. I drank in Mel's story and watched the interesting face of the man telling it.

I pulled the beef from the skewer and dipped it in Davey sauce while Mel told me about the land, the beautiful soil, and the irrigation trenches they dug. The fish and the rice noodles. The children who walked barefoot down the paths between the ditches on their way to school.

I imagined the little kids with their black hair and almond eyes that sparkled when they were given a piece of sugar cane to chew. I imagined a younger version of Mel in a dirty T-shirt and dungarees, with clogs on his feet and a straw hat shading a smile as he looked up from a hoe to encourage a native or grin at a child.

I knew he loved the people, and he loved their country. It wasn't just his own land on the edge of the Alleghenies that he loved, but farms thousands of miles away, and fields that had once been his home. Mel was an earth person, I decided, and that was something I liked. Maybe that came from following my own dad around on the farms he used to call on during my growing-up years. But I think there aren't enough people anymore who value the earth or gain their strength and energy from the ground under their feet.

I remembered the words of Dr. Larch and wondered if Mel would say yes to sustainability but stop short of saying no to agribusiness.

The conversation slowed. Mel asked me some questions to balance the conversational equation. I answered but didn't have any stories half as interesting to tell him as the things he'd told me.

Mel had recently met a woman who was one-fourth Cherokee and a real believer in reincarnation. He and a neighbor had gone to a farm field day and sat across from her at lunchtime. She'd regaled the entire table with talk of spirits walking the earth, the unrest of the dead, and her belief that every life is cosmically connected—unified with the earth, even beyond the grave. I could tell from Mel's first description of the nameless woman and her beliefs that he didn't really go along with her ideas. Still, they held a certain fascination.

"The human race is connected by forces that bring back to the world those who have lived well and gone before," Mel quoted her as saying. "It is the best explanation anyone has for the reason people do things completely out of character. It's why a person will take an interest in something far removed from the interests of anyone in his family. You find people who live in the twentieth century with an overwhelming desire to build a straw and mud house, for instance. Or someone goes on the Internet and finds an old recipe for making soap . . . and the rest is history.

"There's the guy who insists on hunting only with a muzzle loader that he's built with his own hands. There are women who wear sandals year 'round, and men who refuse to take off their shirts, even when they go swimming. There are kids who make up games that were played back in medieval times, and a few women who still do embroidery for hours upon hours, even though most women nowadays never sew a stitch."

According to this Native American matriarch, Mel said, all this shows that people are reincarnated. She herself was once a Chinese princess, which is why she was always begging her husband to stop at the Sizzling Wok and bring home Chinese food for dinner.

Mel made quite a story out of her monologue. She had said the spirits of the dead walk the land at night and knock on doors of homes. "When a couple is in bed and the climate both inside and outside the home is exactly right, that spirit enters into their room. Then a child will be born who has already walked the earth and has the wisdom to live here. We are drawn to that wisdom and it reminds us to live for the future and to cherish the past."

Mel remembered her story well, but I could tell he hadn't bought it. He and his brother, Paulie, had a running joke about it, he said. In fact, Paulie knew about Mel's date with me, and Mel predicted his brother's first question tomorrow would be "Hear anyone knocking last night, Mel?"

I laughed, knowing Mel's response wouldn't be in the affirmative. It had been a great evening, but not in that way.

We savored the last bite of a piece of chocolate cheesecake we had decided to share. In another life, we decided, we were residents of the Netherlands, where we acquired a deep appreciation for dark chocolate combined with rich butterfat. That was the only explanation I could give for Mel spending the extra money on dessert.

As we walked out of the Tavern together, I realized how much I had needed an evening with a man who told great stories and had such a sincere concern for the world beyond Hilldale.

Mel unceremoniously dropped me off near my front door. He stopped the truck and turned to me, making a point of taking my hand in his. He studied it, turned it over to examine my palm, then held it in both of his work-roughened hands for a brief moment.

"I had a wonderful time," he said. His eyes seemed to reach into my heart. "I'll call again sometime. Is that okay?"

"So did I," I answered. "Call anytime. I'd like that." I stood in the driveway and watched him drive off.

"Kairos," I whispered to myself. "A moment of grace. . . . God's time."

Later on I realized I'd never found out what appropriate technology was. And for all I knew, there was only one other person who could answer that question for me. He was several blocks away gaining communication skills and developing empathy.

Fortunately, the class would meet for eight more weeks, except for Thanksgiving week, so there would still be plenty of time to learn the things I too needed to know.

11

Joe arrived before Erika the morning of our next supervisory meeting. "How's it going?" I asked him.

"Not bad, I guess. I didn't expect to be working in rehab when I was in graduate school though."

"I know. It often comes as a surprise after studying all that theory to find yourself out on the street, working day to day as a job coach or leading an employment readiness team. I've heard good reports about your work though. Are you feeling more comfortable than you did at first?

"I think so," he said. "It's just that there's so much to learn, and I worry that if my consumers have a problem I'll be to blame."

"Not at all, Joe. You just do what you can. One of these days we should probably go over some of the signs that your People may need additional medical attention. Don't let me forget."

Erika arrived and the two interns settled into the orange plastic chairs once more for a brief overview of important language considerations. "I'm happy to be able to give you this new material," I told them. "It isn't even in our updated manual yet. It's from the International Association of Psychosocial Rehabilitation Services. We call it IAPSRS, for short," I said, pronouncing the acronym as a word—an odd-sounding one.

"You can read the material in the hand-out yourselves. There's a lot of good stuff there. Basically what I want you to think about is that our language matters more than we realize. If we use language that calls attention to deficits or language that labels People and identifies them with their illness—for instance, saying someone is a schizophrenic—we are using the language of limitation and labels. Remember to always use person-first language: 'a person with a psychiatric disability,' for instance."

"I'm confused about all the terms we use to identify People," Erika said. "I never know what's right."

"I know, it's hard to sort out. But here in this agency, since we aren't giving medical treatment but are concerned with assisting people with day-to-day living skills, rehabilitation, and recovery, we want to carefully avoid deficit language. Certain words go in and out of fashion, but often there's a good reason for making a change. The language we use can actually change our attitudes and eventually our society. Personally, I've never liked the words *client* or *consumer*, but I suppose someone thought they were improvements. I stick with the word *People* whenever possible.

"In fact," I pointed out, "while we habitually refer to what we do as 'case management,' the new guidelines say a more descriptive and less stigmatizing term is 'service coordination' or 'resource coordination.'"

"Hi! I'm Joe and I'm your resource coordinator," Joe said brightly.

"You've got the idea now."

"I see what you mean," said Erika. "After all, People are not *cases*, and I doubt any of us would like to think someone was *managing* us—unless you are hot talent or an athletic wonder."

"Right you are."

Just then there was an intercom buzz from the administrative assistant's office. I picked up my phone. "Someone is here to talk with you. Do you have time to see a person named Darwin?"

"Sure, send him on back."

Joe and Erika stood up. As they were on their way out, Darwin brushed past them and stormed into my office. He closed the door without being invited to and threw himself into the orange chair closest to my desk. Something was certainly very wrong.

Darwin was as angry as I'd ever seen him, and I was momentarily grateful that the front office knew he was there. I considered opening the door or suggesting he ought to let me decide when it needed to be closed, but wisely let it go.

"Look at this!" he demanded, throwing a stapled report onto my desk. "This is really getting me steamed!" he bellowed loudly. "Slave labor. That's what we are. We're just slave labor!"

The paper was some sort of evaluation from his job-training coordinator. Though I was aware of the job programs that were offered, I wasn't familiar with those types of reports or the methods used to generate them.

The first page was a memo that evaluated Darwin's performance at Farnswalters. It was dated the week before and said he had increased to a level of 77 percent, which entitled him to a wage rate of $3.66 starting in December. There was a note stating that if the worker disagreed with the evaluation, he had the right to appeal through the coordinator.

Darwin had signed his name on the line below, and the signature was witnessed by an agency employee. On another line, he had signed a statement saying that he would not appeal the results of the evaluation. I was surprised by the low wage, but I realized that the wages took into account the cost of extra staffing needed for job coaching and program administration.

The next page was an itemized list of tasks Darwin

worked at: outdoor manual labor, greenhouse and plant care, customer assistance. Also listed were requirements such as punctuality, appropriate dress, attention to employee guidelines and regulations, courtesy to customers and other employees, and the like. As I looked over the list, I was impressed that Darwin received top ratings in each category. In fact, none of his marks was below 90 percent.

A key at the bottom of the page included a rating that compared Darwin to other workers with a disability. A mathematical formula that I didn't understand plugged in the 77 percent figure and arrived at the $3.66 hourly rate.

I admitted to Darwin that I didn't understand the system used in the evaluation but told him I'd be happy to look into it further. I complimented him on his high rating, but that just set him off again. He said he didn't understand why, if he was rated 90 percent and above on each task, the final evaluation put him in the 77 percent category. I told him I didn't understand either and promised to find out for him.

Darwin was angry about a lot of things, and all of them involved "the system." The floodgates opened then, and he had my ear. He'd just come from an appointment with a therapist, a trip he'd made using one of his taxi vouchers. The small, rural city of Hilldale didn't have regular bus service, or public transportation of any kind. The vouchers were a compromise to help our People get to their appointments. The counselor is fairly new and was assigned to Darwin by another mental-health agency, so I wasn't even familiar with her.

Ten years ago Darwin was diagnosed SAMI (Substance Abusing Mentally Ill). Using alcohol when on an antidepressant is a bad idea. The mixture can lead to behavior that might land you in jail.

Darwin had been arrested for DUI. He'd paid a fine and

served a term of probation because it was his first offense. Unfortunately, he hadn't learned his lesson, and a few months later he was arrested again. He enrolled in the SAMI program, but after several lapses he was kicked out. The solution was to assign him to a substance-abuse counselor instead of the mental-health counselor he'd been seeing for several years.

"Where do they get these people?" Darwin demanded. "It seems like if you can't get a job anywhere, or don't know what else to do, you end up being a counselor."

I felt bad about what he'd said, but it was easy to understand his anger. Darwin was a bright, intelligent person. Workers in the public system were often young—fresh out of graduate school. The system was a good place to get the supervised hours they needed for credentials. Once they've passed their licensure exams, however, they often move on to other things.

"I was complaining to her that I have only $4.50 left to get me through to the end of the month. I have bills to pay, a house to heat. And this young lady looks me in the eye and says to me, 'Well, if you wouldn't spend all your check on beer, you'd have enough to get you through the month.' Well, let me tell you, that really ticked me off! How does she know what I spend my money on? Even if she can prove I've been drinking—which she can't—how does she know someone didn't buy me a beer. I guess I was pretty fed up and told the friggin' baby girl off, because the next thing I knew, she told me to get out of her office.

"Sometimes I feel like once you're in my shoes, you're a marked man. You can't win, no matter what you do. They've got your number; they're out to get you."

Darwin stopped to take a breath and I struggled for the right words. "I'm sorry you have so many problems, Darwin. It doesn't seem fair, does it?"

I didn't approve of his drinking. I had thought it was

over and done with, but the simple fact was that in our society, it's more acceptable to have a drinking problem than to be branded mentally ill. And I'd seen some newer studies that showed how drinking and bipolar disorder are often related, perhaps because of a particular brain chemistry.

"No. No way!" Darwin continued. "The other week I went out to Booneville to give my little nephew his birthday gift. I got him this huge blow-up frog at a yard sale. His folks asked me to stop by for a piece of cake. Afterward I'm walking down the street on my way to the phone booth. I have a walking stick in my hand and I poke a couple of garbage bags that are sitting out along the curb. And here, just down the way, sits the Booneville police cruiser. The officer is watching, and next thing you know he's flashing his lights and telling me to get in the cruiser. Says I was breaking a village ordinance by tampering with the garbage. Now, you tell me, would they have stopped you if you'd been out walking down the street?"

Darwin might have been manic, even paranoid. It was hard to tell, but I thought otherwise. He was staying on the topic, which happened to be his perceived unjust treatment at the hands of the mental-health system. I had no choice but to think that on the face of it, he had some legitimate gripes.

Darwin looked up from his boots. I felt deeply sorry for him, almost a feeling of pity, which I realized wasn't helpful. His story had wormed its way into my heart and the professional lingo didn't seem accessible or appropriate. I sat there with him in silence, recognizing in a new way how when a person suffers, as he has, even small injustices are magnified. So how must these things make him feel?

The air in my closed-up office felt hot and stale—more so because Darwin's clothes reeked of cigarette smoke. I thought about how the price of cigarettes had risen recently. More of Darwin's disposable income will be "going up in smoke."

He stopped talking and looked over at me. He had tears in his eyes. I thought about what a struggle his life had been—and what a struggle it remained.

"You're having a hard time of it," I said. "It isn't easy, I know. And the system that is supposed to be helping you sometimes makes it even harder. That's not the way it should work."

Darwin grew silent and nodded. I knew he heard what I was saying and he recognized how *I* had heard *him*. Suddenly I felt so drawn to Darwin, one of my People, who was just another human being—a hurting, intelligent human being who was trying to do his best against great odds. I stood up and walked around my desk to face him and said, "I'm sorry, Darwin. So sorry. Things should be better than this."

And then, behind my closed door, I bent over and gave him a hug as he sat there in my guest chair. He was surprised and a little taken aback. I was surprised too because I'm not a "huggy" person. I wondered how long it had been since anyone had said a few kind words to him—sincerely kind words—and hugged him.

Many times I had said things that sounded kind and caring, but this time was different. Though I'd heard stories from People who felt misunderstood and betrayed by a system that was supposed to be there to help, I'd caught a glimpse of how hard Darwin's life really was. All those years he'd been part of the system, yet there he was, still being looked at in the same way though he'd made great strides in his recovery. It should have been possible to break out of the prison he was in. It *was* a kind of apartheid. Yes, I believed it was.

I placed a stack of folders sitting in front of me into my in-box and sat back in my chair. I opened my top desk drawer and got out a bag of chocolate-covered caramels and handed one to Darwin. I unwrapped another one for myself. We sat there chewing the sticky candy and thinking about what to say next.

But words didn't seem necessary just then.

12

THE FOLLOWING TUESDAY I was off for Veterans Day, and
Rhonda invited me over to her place. It seemed unusual to
show up on her doorstep to socialize on a weekday. So
much of my life happened "out there," at restaurants, coffee
shops, lectures, readings, and conferences. When I wasn't
circulating in those places I was with my People, in their
homes or in my car.

Rhonda had suggested I bring walking shoes.
Remembering our springtime hike in the forest, I looked forward to a walk in the fields and woods behind her house.

Rhonda and Dale lived in a home they had built on a
lot carved from what Dale once called "unfarmable" land
previously owned by his parents. It's a cookie-cutter ranch,
but I forgot that when I saw the plants everywhere, perenni-
als of all kinds, although most of them were in the dormant
phase that day. Near Rhonda's front door I noticed a huge
bed where clumps of low-lying alyssum escaped the frost.
Towering above were tall black-eyed Susans, which had
been hit by Jack Frost and were black, leaves and all.

Rhonda and Katie, her black-and-white, long-haired
cat, met me at the door. They looked ready for the outdoors. Katie followed us as if she were a dog. Rhonda said
she wanted to take me on a hike around the perimeter of a
pasture. But first we crossed through a low-lying area that
was squishy underfoot. Someone had put down planks,
which were slick and beginning to rot underneath, but they
got us over the damp areas—a boardwalk of sorts.

"I needed this today," I said to Rhonda.

"I thought you looked troubled the last few times I've seen you. What's happening in your life these days?"

I considered how to accept her invitation to self-revelation. "I don't know. I can't explain it. But it seems I'm being pulled in a direction I didn't plan to go—don't even want to go. Almost like I am *meant* to go somewhere I wasn't intending." It sounded vague to my own ears and yet Rhonda seemed to understand.

"Is it like a journey you are taking? Are you feeling lost?"

"Well, yes. Or like I'm being pulled into a river and I'm powerless over the current."

"That's a good description of the beginning of an awakening."

"Awakening?"

"You will become more awake now to the movement of Spirit in your life. Once you start to notice, you'll see it everywhere. And life becomes an adventure. But be ready for some hard things. It may not be easy."

"We sometimes tell our People life is a journey. God knows theirs aren't easy!"

"Yes, a journey, or a river that carries you along. Get in the river—and swim."

At that exact moment Rhonda lost her footing and fell sprawling into the soggy creek bed. I realized she wasn't hurt and helped her up as we started laughing. It felt so good to laugh with her.

"I'm having a lot of strange things happen to me," I continued.

"I know," she says, making me wonder what she knew. But surely she couldn't be aware of my trip to Mel's farm or the "I love you" I'd blurted out to Darwin, or the way I'd started crying over his scrapbooks, or the hug I'd given him.

"I have a lot of *feelings* all of a sudden," I told Rhonda as we moved across the steep upgrade that led us to a hay-field of stubble and short alfalfa ends.

"Feelings?"

"Well, you know . . . it's what you might call passion. But not in the sense of falling in love!" I added quickly. "There's a lot of intensity about things. Sometimes little things. I'm crying too, about small stuff."

"I think that goes with it," Rhonda said gently. "Be open. Explore the relationship between passion and trust. Be ready to let go."

Passion and trust didn't seem to connect for me at all. "How can I face another winter when I feel like this?" That's what I'd *really* been thinking lately. I'd say I must have some brain chemistry problem. Another bad bout of Seasonal Affective Disorder, or a lingering dysthymia. Passion and trust? Now that's a different take on things.

"Speaking of passion," I said, changing the subject, "I did have a dinner date the other night."

"Really? With who?"

"Oh, a guy I met the other weekend. Kind of different though. Mel Martin. He's taking one of the Family Support classes."

Rhonda nodded her approval. "Hey, that's great. He's a good guy. I went to school with him—in fact went to church with him too—the whole time I was growing up. Think you'll hear from him again?"

"Well, yes, I hope so. He seems kind of shy. But now he'll be coming to Hilldale every week for the class. In fact, that's when we had dinner—before his first one." I felt as if I could chatter on, but checked myself. It wouldn't do to have Rhonda see me too excited about this.

"Well, whatever you do, don't start diagnosing him and trying to help him," she said with a grin. "Just be yourself!"

"It's usually me I diagnose. But I can't help it. That *is* myself. I diagnose and help. Me, help-er. Others, help-ee. 'Cept you, of course."

"Not this time," Rhonda said firmly. "Be a good friend to that man. And, Angie, I was thinking about what you said the other day about art, painting, and so on. Why don't you get some paint or do some kind of artwork? You could even make something to put in the art show for Mental Health Month."

She had a point. I often thought it would be nice if agency staff would put things in the show. Usually it was only the clients who showed their work, but there was no reason some of the rest of us couldn't contribute.

"I don't know. I guess art is just something I quit doing a long time ago. It seems sort of frivolous to spend time painting when there's so much need in the world, so many people who need so much help. So much suffering and so few people working to alleviate it. Besides, my stuff never looks right to me. The last time I tried to paint, it ended up face to the wall in the attic. Maybe my art is to help someone else have the opportunity to do it."

Rhonda didn't reply, and I sensed she disagreed.

"You have to see this," she said as she guided me to a small building at the edge of a farmhouse lawn. "This is an old springhouse."

She opened a door on creaky hinges, and we stepped inside a cool room with stone walls and a cement floor. There was a large fireplace with a wide, bare hearth. The walls were whitewashed. Across the end was a trough made of rough cement embedded with tiny stones. Water flowed from a mineral-encrusted pipe into the trough, which was full.

"It's an artesian well," Rhonda said. "Years ago people put their perishables in here to keep them cold."

I put my hand in the water and lifted it out quickly. Very cold.

"The water comes from deep in the earth, pushed up by its own force. You can't stop it easily. You'd have to cap the pipe. It's a natural spring."

"Why doesn't it run over?"

"There's a drain in the side of the trough. It will never overflow, but it will never dry up either."

I thought of the soggy section of earth we had walked over and saw now where that dampness had come from.

"I think of this as God's love," Rhonda told me as she splashed her hand in the water. "Let justice roll down like water. And righteousness like an ever-flowing stream." Those are the words of Amos the prophet. I've always liked Amos. He was a shepherd. A farmer.

She took her wet hand and cupped a bit of the cold water into it. She pulled me toward her with the other. "I sprinkle you with the water of love. May your passion grow and your trust be renewed. You are God's beloved. Go now with Spirit."

Her words seemed to gush like the water, and I felt the cool dampness on my forehead where she had splashed me. It was a spontaneous ritual, a kind of baptism, playful and meaningful at the same time. A rite of initiation I could carry with me to remember this day.

❦

On the way home I thought about painting. Maybe Rhonda had a point. What she didn't know was, years ago I could sit for hours in a cold room, oils at my elbow, unable to tear myself away from the canvas. Before me the paint swirled with the stroke of my hand, completely apart from my will. Passion flowed from my brush in those days.

I would sit as if in meditation, often for hours and hours, long past bedtime. Sometimes I couldn't sleep and got up early in the morning to paint. I didn't need sleep when that happened. Sleep became secondary to the creative spirit that surged in my veins. I remembered how, after painting for a few hours, I would leave the easel, and everything around me was extraordinarily vivid—brighter and crisper, somehow.

Before I got to Hilldale, I came to one of the ubiquitous detours that seem to plague the township roads during warmer months, as local crews try to shore up the aging bridges. The signs were easy to follow, though, and I found myself entering Hilldale from a side road I seldom traveled. "Maybe there is a reason for this detour," I thought, using the logic I imagined Rhonda would use. "I will see where this takes me. Maybe I'm *supposed* to be on this road."

The street ahead seemed unusually full of parked cars. There was a yard sale going on. A big yard sale, despite the late season. It had been a long time since I'd gone to a yard sale, except with of one of my People, who sometimes used them as a form of entertainment and a place to buy affordable knickknacks and furnishings.

I pulled over and walked toward the trampled lawn, surveying the piles of folded clothes, cowboy boots, odd wall sconces, and stained Pyrex ware. There was a row of beat-up cheap furniture and a lamp that made me think "art deco." I felt foolish for stopping but decided to take one loop through the garage, just in case.

I spied a piece of luggage in a back corner. It reminded me of the old train case I'd had as a girl. For years I'd kept it on a closet shelf, stuffed with Barbies and all the accessories. I had no idea what became of it. Maybe it was in Mom's attic. She'd keep things like that.

My curiosity aroused, I opened the case and drew in

my breath. It was full of art supplies: brushes, pastels, a few bottles of acrylics, glazes and other bottles of things I recognized. I noted the word "Spirits" on one bottle and knew instinctively that these were for me. I picked it up; this case was mine.

"I guess I'll take this," I told the heavy-set woman sitting behind a flimsy card table with her hand on a metal cash box.

"Oh, you found the art supplies," she said. "I was hoping someone would get those. They were my mother's. She died last summer from cancer. It was horrible. A lot of this stuff is hers. I hope they're still okay. She didn't paint for a long time. Some of her canvases are in the basement. I haven't even looked at all of it."

"Oh, I'm so sorry about your mother," I said. "I'll try to make good use of the paints. I promise. I used to paint and I was thinking of trying again."

"Did you see, there's oils down in the bottom too?"

"No, I didn't really notice. Looks like there's a lot of stuff in here."

"Just a minute." The big woman stood up, pushed some strands of hair out of her face, and tucked them under her ball cap. "I've got some canvases you can have. Can you hold on a minute? I'll get them for you."

She closed the cash box and carried it with her inside the house. When she returned she had several canvases stretched on their frames under her arm.

"How much do I owe you?" I asked.

"Oh, let me see. . . . How does ten dollars sound?"

"Is that all? These are worth a lot more than that."

"No, that's all right. Mom would have wanted an artist to have it. She went through a stage where she really painted a lot and then—I don't know what happened—she just stopped. There's a real nice picture in there she kind of started and then quit on. Maybe you'll finish it for her."

I carried the case and the canvases to my car and placed them in the trunk. It was getting colder, so I pulled my fleece jacket around me. I drove down the street, still not sure where I was going. Before long I recognized the west side of Hilldale Medical Center on my left.

I was back in familiar territory.

13

SOME OF LIFE'S most meaningful experiences are lived in the company of a good horse. Sunday morning was chilly, but I had promised Mel I'd go riding with him. I'd made the early drive to his place in about an hour, much less than before. I wondered how the time had slipped away on that first trip, as if it had taken a different form. *Kairos* maybe?

As a child I'd enjoyed riding at a nearby stable, but it had been years since I'd been in the saddle. Still, like so many other things, if you've learned it as a child, you never really forget. I was looking forward to being with Mel, who had called me again with the excuse of letting me know how much he was learning in Family Support Class.

The air was still pungent with harvest scents and the damp morning. I took a deep breath as I stepped out of my car and felt a peaceful sense of homecoming. I zipped up my hooded sweatshirt. The weather seemed perfect for being outdoors. Now all I had to do was remember how to ride.

Mel joined me on the porch. "Don't worry," he said when I expressed some qualms about riding again. He closed the screen door softly, and I noticed his appreciative look in my direction as he pulled on his boots.

"Last time I was here, I didn't even see your horses," I told him.

"They were probably out in the pasture. As long as there's some grass left, we just let them on pasture. They're happier out there than penned up any day."

We stopped by the stable, which was in the basement

of an outbuilding—a cement-block garage—to pick up the bridles. The place was small, with just two stalls for the horses and an open area stacked with bales of hay, a few bags of horse feed, and a saw horse with a couple of well-worn western saddles thrown over it. Even in the absence of its residents, Sugar and Lightning, the stable held that familiar horsy smell. It made me feel more at home than I'd felt in years.

Mel was in a talkative mood. It usually takes me a while to wake up in the morning, so I just listened while he told me about the horses. His favorite—the one he thought of as his—was Sugar. In retrospect, Mel said, the horse was poorly named. In fact the two steeds should have had their names reversed, but Mel's wife, Loretta, had named Sugar, the large, trim sorrel, the day he arrived on the farm. The name stuck despite their later discovery that he was fast, exceptionally well trained, and anything but a sweetheart sometimes.

Mel had bought Sugar from an elderly horse trader who regularly made trips to Texas and bought culled ranch horses, which he then trucked to Ohio. Almost before the horses were off the truck, the trader was advertising them in the *Farm & Dairy*. Loretta had always dreamed of owning a horse, so soon after they were married and moved onto the farm, they started looking. When they answered the ad, Sugar was still recovering from the trip, but they'd recognized a good horse under the scruffy appearance.

"You should have seen him," Mel told me. "He was matted with dirt, and there were patches of hide showing through where his coat was completely gone. His head and legs were scraped up something awful, but I liked the narrow blaze down his long nose—and I'd have recognized the origin of that neck anywhere.

"Look at his small hooves," he said as he lifted each foot

to check for loose shoes or injuries. "That is always something to pay attention to in a riding horse. My final test was to look inside his mouth." Mel demonstrated by tugging on Sugar's lower jaw, exposing an impressive set of choppers.

"From the look of his teeth, I could tell he still had a few years left in him. I took one look at him and said to myself, 'Thoroughbred.' Sure enough, I was right. The ol' horse trader tells me this specimen came straight off the King Ranch in Texas. 'Likely story,' I say to myself, but I let the guy go on about how he gets most of his horses from the King Ranch and a couple of other ranches in that part of Texas.

"The horses from King Ranch are always trained best, he tells me, and this one came with an exceptional recommendation from the cowboys down there. I ask about the horse's rough appearance and the trader assures me that in a few days I'll never believe the change. It's just that the trip is hard on the animals. 'Right,' I'm thinking. 'Thanks to you and your money-grubbing ways.' But I don't see anything that makes me change my mind. I'm sold, in spite of the nasty look of his coat and the obvious need for some good nutrition."

It turned out Sugar is really half thoroughbred and half quarter horse. "There could be worse combinations," Mel observed.

I realized now why I'd missed seeing the horses last time. The pasture was in the opposite direction from the way we went when we hiked across the farm. I was warming up, and Mel's story about Sugar had managed to distract me from my fears about riding.

Mel gave a soft whistle. Lightning came running up to the steel gate and nuzzled his hand. He deftly grabbed the halter and pulled it over the horse's ears while sliding the bridle on almost simultaneously. He slipped the bit into Lightning's mouth and hooked the reins over the gate.

Lightening, a chestnut with a large white star on his nose and four white forelegs, stamped impatiently and whinnied. He looked friendly, and it was obvious he was shorter than Sugar, who was circling the pasture, trying to ignore Mel. We stood there alternately rubbing Lightning's damp nose and watching the wild one beyond the gate.

"Lightning isn't near the horse Sugar is," Mel said, "but he's still nice to ride. He's yours for today. I'm not sure you'd want Sugar if you haven't been on a horse in as long as you're saying." I nodded, but couldn't help admiring Sugar, who tossed his head and kicked up his heels as he made a wider circle. He was beautiful, and I couldn't imagine him being in the shape Mel had just described.

Mel jumped lightly over the gate and walked in the direction of Sugar while I held the other bridle. It took some coaxing, but Sugar was soon convinced a morning ride might be all right and headed toward the gate. We led the horses back to the stable to get the saddles.

"I had to end up getting Lightning for Loretta," Mel told me. "As soon as I rode Sugar, I realized he wasn't the right kind of horse for a first-time rider. That time, I didn't buy from a horse trader. We got Lightning from a quarter-horse breeder over in Carey County. He's well trained too, but nothing like Sugar."

Sugar was the quintessential riding horse, perfectly neck-reined so a rider had only to lightly lay the rein on his neck and he'd turn. A slight pull on the bit, and he stopped immediately. He could stand for as long as you wished in one place if his reins were touching the ground, and he had an appealing canter that reminded me of a childhood rocking horse.

I would probably ride Sugar someday, but right then I was wary of that spirit. And he probably knew it. Mel was right. I had to get my horse sense back by riding Lightning first.

I was thinking Mel still hadn't said much about Loretta. Maybe he read my mind, because just then he said, "Almost as soon as we'd moved onto the farm, Loretta started complaining about her leg a lot. The doctors recommended vascular surgery, and she was all for it. Anything to be able to go riding. That's what she really wanted. She just loved these horses.

"I know getting them did bring her a lot of joy, even though she never got to ride much. Maybe that's why I still keep them both here—to remind me of her.

"It's too bad they don't get ridden nearly enough anymore. Sometimes the neighbor girls come over and ask to ride. They're in that adolescent stage when they love horses more than boys. They're good handlers, though. Sunday morning before church is my favorite time to ride. It's almost my *only* time to ride. Sometimes I think it's better than church.

"It will be nice to have someone with me for a change. Loretta died two years ago last Wednesday." Mel looked over at me again. I dipped into the deep-blue glint of his eyes, which seemed deeper and brighter than the early-morning sky. They lit up when he talked about his horses. He seemed at peace talking about Loretta too, and I wondered how he could so easily converse about her. Their life together must have seemed to him such a short time ago.

"How can you just talk about her like that?" I asked him without feeling at all self-conscious. There he was, walking back from the pasture *with me* leading those same two horses, and he seemed to enjoy my company. I didn't hear any pain in his voice, just a tinge of sadness. But when I thought of the sudden, unexpected death of Mel's dear wife, I knew he must feel pain, especially with us and the horses there together like that.

My heart ached for Mel as he told me about how she'd

died so suddenly from a blood clot two days after surgery. She should have healed without incident, and they would have gone on with their lives as a couple of dairy farmers.

"Was she Mennonite too?" I asked him, suspecting he'd have married someone of his own faith.

"Oh, yes, she was. She was such a beautiful woman, Angie. So gracious and loving. She loved children and wanted to have a big garden. That's why I've got this truck patch. And she was talented too. I don't think there was much of any homemaking thing she couldn't do. She sewed and baked and put away food in the can cupboard and freezer. It was her who made me want to settle down. She wrote to me all through my years in Laos. I still have all those letters."

Mel seemed at peace, but I thought the grief must still linger. "How can you be so accepting of this?" I asked. "Aren't you angry at God for taking her?"

"Oh, I don't think of it that way at all," Mel said. "I know God allows things to happen to us. Everything is for a reason. We can't question God's ways. We don't understand, but he knows what is best. 'All things work together for the good of them that love the Lord and are called according to his purpose.'"

I didn't agree with or, to be honest, understand that kind of thinking. But I didn't know how to put into words what I *did* believe, if anything.

"I know she's in heaven with the angels and Jesus, on the right hand of God," Mel continued. "I wouldn't wish her back to *this*."

For my part, I didn't think *this* was too shabby. I remained silent, and I let our theological differences resonate in rhythm to the comfortable plodding of horse hooves on the sod.

After we saddled up, we took the horses to the woods

and followed a stream up to his favorite rocky ravine. Mel lived in wonderful country for horseback riding. Although it was mostly a patchwork of large fields and fertile farmland, there were also scattered wooded areas on the hillsides. Mel was able to avoid the area's few fences because he knew the right paths. We wandered over several acres, across the neighboring farms, and saw everything from vantage points never possible in a car, moving easily over terrain that would have been tedious on foot.

As the sun rose higher over the stubbly cornfield, Mel and I headed south. Lightning proved to be a trustworthy mount, solid and predictable under me. I relaxed into the well-worn saddle Mel had cinched securely for me. I felt the familiar rhythm of a horse under me, carrying me to places that allow us to escape the ordinary. On horseback, we were high enough off the ground to see things differently.

"I have a place I want to show you," Mel told me after a long but comfortable silence. We had been riding companionably along a fencerow that was allowed to stay wild. We saw signs of wildlife everywhere. As I rode behind Mel, he sometimes pointed to the ground below, or to a tree, or off into the distance. I saw some of what he was pointing out, but other sights escaped or eluded me. I soaked in the cool beauty of the morning and its peace.

I watched Mel sitting easily in the saddle and thought about the goodness in him, how he loved those fields and fencerows and the creatures that lived there. I began to feel the passion I'd spoken of to Rhonda. It was a wild energy to which I was unaccustomed and had tried a few days ago to describe for her.

Again we were on the lane where we walked last time I was there. Ahead of me Mel pointed to the dusty tracks. "Coyote," he said. Like us, they had left stories as they passed this way.

The fields led us to a farm set almost as high as Mel's and back several hundred feet off the county road. We crossed over a narrow, dirt road and followed a creek for a short distance, then trotted across a large, open field. The alfalfa and timothy was crunchy underfoot, and the feathery tops must have tickled the horses' ankles.

We gave them rein, and they charged forward in a full gallop. I felt the wind in my hair and the cool morning air. My face tingled and my ears hurt, but the air felt strong and energizing as it charged into my lungs. My leg muscles tensed slightly as they hugged Lightning's round torso. Riding again felt wonderful.

We approached another wooded area, and Mel slowed Sugar to a trot once more. I rode up beside him, and he began to tell me about our destination, God's Hollow. I laughed at the name, which seemed like an effort to create a sacred place from a spot that was probably once called Devil's Hollow. I said as much to Mel and he confirmed my suspicion.

"People around here are pretty religious, you know?" he said. "It wouldn't do to let the devil have a place like this. Wait till you see it."

We guided the horses through a break in the evergreens that spread out in both directions directly in front of us. "What are these trees?" I asked Mel as I took in their pungent fragrance and looked up at the feathery fronds creating a roof over us.

"Hemlocks," he replied with reverence.

We reined in and sat breathlessly taking in the wild beauty below. We were on the rim of a sheer drop of eighty feet or so, with a creek at the bottom.

Following a cow path, we descended over a hogback to the bottom of God's Hollow. Some of the hemlocks were up to three feet across! I would have never guessed that such a place existed in our part of the country. Further east in the Appalachians, maybe, but not here. The horses' hoof beats were muted as we traveled on a bed of evergreen needles through the natural cathedral. Colorful birds were at home there: cardinals, chickadees, and some I couldn't identify. We stopped next to the creek, dismounted, and let the horses drink.

While they rested, Mel told me about the hemlocks. "These are excellent habitat for wildlife," he said. Besides the cover the hemlock provided, deer, ruffed grouse, and rabbits ate the buds and the sprays of tender needles. Several species of birds fed on the seeds from the small hemlock cones. On the knoll above the rim of the gorge was one of the few places in Ohio where trailing arbutus thrived, Mel told me. It bloomed delicate, pink blossoms in early spring.

My guide promised to bring me back in the spring to find hepatica and wild trillium, which grows from a bulb and was even now nestled under the floor of the hardwood forest that banked this rocky rim, waiting for spring. Trillium must be cousin to Mel's garlic bulbs that were resting dormant in the garden next to his house across the fields.

We rode the long length of the gorge, following the creek until we reached open country once again. At the top of the gorge we stopped at an informal lookout spot that seemed to invite us. We sat side by side on Sugar and Lightning and gazed across the natural beauty, so hidden from the world.

"God's Hollow," I whispered, almost to myself.

"Yeah," replied Mel, in a similar tone of reverence.

We drank in the Sabbath silence. And then I felt myself starting to cry again. Mel looked toward me, his face gentle, his eyes kind.

"What are you thinking, Angie?" he asked.

"This place is so beautiful. It makes me want to ask questions. Where is God? Why do so many people in our world suffer? Why is there so much trouble—for my People and for us? Why do those we love always seem to leave us, just when we begin to trust that they will always be there?"

This time it was more than eyes brimming over. I was truly crying as I reached into my sweatshirt pocket for a tissue.

Mel tossed Sugar's reins to the ground and dismounted. He came over to me and reached up to take Lightning's reins from my hands. Then he held my arm firmly and guided me off the horse. He cupped my cold cheeks in his warm palms and his blue eyes locked onto mine.

"I don't know, Angie. I don't know," he said to me, and after a moment, "Let's sit here a bit." He gestured toward a log that had long ago been placed there as a seat for watching the view below us. Mel tied Lightning's reins loosely to a sapling.

I stood alternately sobbing and sniffling. Mel wrapped his arms around me, and I rested my head on his chest. I could smell the farm in his worn coat and feel the strength of his arms holding me. His hands pressed into my back, which was shaking with the sobs I was trying to suppress.

"It's okay, Angie. Go ahead and cry. Let it all out."

It seemed I couldn't stop crying, and Mel made no effort to stop me. He held me for a long time, until I became calmer. I pulled away and dabbed at my eyes with the soggy tissue. Mel pulled a red hanky from his pocket and handed it to me. It smelled of aftershave. I smiled weakly through my tears.

He pulled me down onto the natural bench, where we sat drinking in the view. Then he began to speak quietly. "I don't know the answers to your questions, Angie. I've asked all of them too, more than once. I've felt despair. I've wondered about so many things. But I've also gradually come to enjoy the beauty of life, even with its disappointments and despair. This place, maybe more than any, makes me know there is someone who cares for us.

"I find God out here in the natural world as much as anywhere. 'I lift up mine eyes unto the hills from whence cometh my help.' The ancient hemlocks, wildflowers, the wings of meadowlarks and soaring hawks. They lift us with them if we watch.

"When I look out over this gorge and see its beauty, I find beauty in the rest of life too. That stream down there—it flows out to my fields, watering the healing grasses that renew the soil. And the wild geese that fly overhead honking seem to sing a hymn. 'This is the day the Lord has made. Let us rejoice and be glad in it.'"

I was getting used to Mel's old-fashioned Bible verses scattered into our lives as if they were part of it. Come to think of it, Rhonda did that too, sometimes.

"I know it can seem like it's a harsh world we live in, Angie, but I also know that when we have the Spirit of the Creator within us, we can touch the holy in ourselves and in those we meet.

"I guess for me it's not so much a matter of doing the right things, or believing the right things, or even asking the right questions. It is a matter of believing there is a Creator who is always at work. We have moments every day that open to the creation of what's to come. That's really all we have. Just today."

"A moment of grace," I said. *Kairos.*

"You asked about Loretta, about losing her and how I made peace. Maybe that's when I stopped working so hard and began to listen to what life is trying to say to me—to live *with* the questions."

I nodded and sniffled. I had nothing to say. But I'd

heard Mel's testimony to life. When I thought about it later, I knew I'd seen this message in the way he lived his life. Now I understood. I reached for his hand and snuggled my own into his warm palm. That was my response. His, a squeeze back. We sat a long time gazing over the valley below us.

$$\tilde{e}$$

The sun was higher in the sky when we climbed back on the horses. I was surprised to notice that my shoulder didn't hurt, in spite of the cool, damp morning. "If it does later," I thought, "it will be well worth it anyway."

"Let's go back to the house and make some breakfast," Mel suggested. "I'll skip church today. We'll have our own."

"Maybe we already have," I said.

"Just don't tell my mother that. If I'm not mistaken, she'll be calling this afternoon to find out where I was. Of course she's just worried about me, that I might be sick, you know."

"What will you tell her?" I asked.

"Probably the truth," said Mel. "The horses wandered clear over to God's Hollow."

A silence set in as we rode back, and I remembered something—a kind of therapy I'd heard of recently. It was used for adolescents who had missed out on the essential bonding experience needed by small children if they are to develop normally.

When children miss out on the hugs, lap-sitting, and kindness that all children need, they sometimes grow up troubled and "at risk." People who grow to adulthood without this essential bonding have an empty well, a bottomless pit that never gets enough love.

A key to helping youth recover and move forward was

found when they experienced love from a compassionate human who knew how to behave in caring ways. Specially trained therapists spent time with them in a comfortable room, simply holding them and hugging them. That's how God seals up the bottom of the well. Until then, the life spring can never push to the top and overflow in loving relationships with others.

Rhonda would like to know about holding therapy. I thought that maybe I would tell her next time we talked because, being with Mel, I was beginning to understand how it works.

14

I SAVORED THE VIEW from the top of the gorge, and it took me into the next week with enthusiasm and renewed energy. Someone had understood and heard my deepest questions about life. Although I didn't completely understand or even remember all of Mel's words, I knew that something important had happened between us. More and more he was becoming a compassionate presence in my life. He cared about my questions.

It felt like an awakening to me. Maybe that's why I didn't tell anyone about it. I thought of telling Rhonda, but we didn't talk that entire week. I also didn't tell Darwin. It would have been too awkward to let him know I'd gone to Mel's farm without him. I'd suggested inviting him, but Mel hadn't seemed to want Darwin included; he only had two horses, he'd said.

I was still basking in the glow of the day before, feeling grateful that someone had finally paid attention to me and my needs. First Rhonda, and now Mel. At Monday's staff meeting, I sat at the large conference table, glad I wasn't directly across from our director, Barbara. I watched her for clues that she might have somehow caught wind of my trespasses of social-worker ethics, compounding with complexity as the weeks wore on. But she seemed completely unaware.

That didn't stop me from sliding into feelings of guilt and remorse as I sat there watching our staff slowly assemble with their mugs of coffee and tea. I was one of the most experienced and best-qualified agency workers. I should have known better and should have maintained the boundaries of my and Darwin's respective roles as social worker and consumer. I covered by jumping into the discussion with uncharacteristic enthusiasm.

"We've got to start seeing our People as *real people* and take their needs and questions seriously," I said. "I'm not talking about the usual need for apartment furnishings or dental work. I'm talking about their need to feel that they are being heard when they start talking about the things that matter to them.

"Every one of our People have things that matter to them," I continued. I was thinking of Darwin and his scrapbooks and Kyra's artwork. "It might not always be the things *we* think are important. I have one Person who takes great care of his collections of stuff, which a lot of other people might view as junk. In his mind these things have real significance.

"We need to try to understand what things mean to our People. We need to further draw them out and get them talking. If they trust a case manager, that's a start toward trusting others."

One or two of my co-workers nodded their heads in agreement. A few others had vacant stares or made doodles on their notepads. I knew they didn't get it. I wished that I could do a better job of communicating my ideas, but maybe some people just didn't *want* to hear what I was saying. I wasn't ready to give specific examples from either my own life or from the lives of my People, although that could have clarified things.

When Barbara pulled me aside at the end of the meeting and said, "I've been wanting to discuss something with you, Angie," my heart sank. Perhaps she *had* found out about my indiscretions. I followed her down the hall and up two flights of stairs to her comfortable office on the second floor. She carefully shut the door behind us. Barbara's office was uncluttered and well decorated. It was designed to be a haven, but I was too nervous to feel calmed by it.

I sank into an overstuffed guest chair, and she offered me a cup of coffee from a small pot on a table in the corner of her spacious room. She sat on the nearby love seat upholstered in a cool green and magenta floral print.

As it turned out, instead of calling me in to reprimand me, she'd been impressed with my words on behalf of our clients and told me so. I was relieved and flattered to be noticed by Barbara, who often seemed aloof and self-absorbed. "I don't have any bone to pick with you or anything, Angie. I've been thinking of a project I wanted to initiate, and when you talked about consumers during the meeting, I got to thinking you might be the person to take on this project.

"As you may, or may not know, we've been given a special grant to work on an innovative project that would expand our outcome-based treatment planning. I've been exploring various ideas being tried around the state. I sense you'd have a feel for this kind of thing. I noticed that particularly in the way you've worked with Darwin, getting him involved in the job-training program and moving him away from his more negative behaviors. There's been a big reduction in his wandering around. Psycho-social rehab says his socialization skills improved dramatically after you started working with him."

I smiled at Barbara and pictured Darwin hefting huge forkfuls of manure onto the manure spreader and chattering away to Buster. There was plenty of truth in what Barbara was saying, including the pleasant conversation we'd had the other day about a whole eclectic collection of subjects.

I was relieved Barbara didn't know about my relationship with Darwin's uncle, and especially how I'd met him. But she *had* heard about Darwin's improved condition. In those moments I thought about how we really need to call this what it is: recovery. People do recover if we help them put the right mixture of support into their lives and don't complicate things with bad housing, insufficient support services, and outdated medications. I considered reminding Barbara of this, but thought she might take offense. Besides, she was setting the agenda as she continued to outline a new assignment.

"I'd like you to visit three sites in Ohio where consumer-based activities are being initiated, and then present a report and possibly also some recommendations at a future staff meeting. After this initial report, other staff will be asked to join you in a work group that will review your report and explore other recovery-based materials. Once we formulate the plan, we'll run it by the board of directors for their input.

"Your assignment, should you choose to accept it . . ." Barbara continued with a smile, "is to try to come up with a plan for some kind of program that would"—she lifted a stapled-together report from her desk and read from it in a faintly mocking tone—"utilize the input of consumers to establish outcome-based initiatives that will further reduce recidivism and inpatient hospital utilization factors."

I knew what she wanted. "So you'd like me to visit these places with a couple of our People and then offer suggestions for ways we could incorporate elements of their programs into ours?" I asked.

"Yes," Barbara said. "We need more ways to guide consumers into the process. After all, our People are the ones who can tell us what works, what they need to stay well, and what motivates them to stick with a program, manage their illness, and stay on their medications. We know that the more knowledgeable, skilled, and motivated a consumer is, the more likely he or she will be to recover."

Now Barbara had used the word *recovery*.

"So the key is to engage People in things that will allow them to find success," she continued. "We have to provide education and encourage skill-building. As you mentioned in staff meeting, helping our People identify activities that allow them to be successful and helping them set manageable goals that they track on a daily basis are part of what it will take.

"Until recently, the word *recovery* is more often used in speaking about treatment for drug and alcohol addiction. But recent literature shows that *recovery* also describes the healing process for a person with a psychiatric disorder —even someone identified as having a disabling condition. As you know, we're sometimes surprised by the outcomes."

I nodded.

"The key is, responsibility must begin to lie with each individual, not with a system or a case manager, and that's what I heard you hint at in staff meeting today."

"I've been thinking," I said. "Sometimes what looks like success for us may not be. What it takes to make *me* a success may not always allow me to be my best, for that matter."

"I'm not sure what you're trying to say."

"Well, maybe some of our People are as close to success as we are, but in a different way."

"For instance?"

"Well, take Kyra, one of my People. She lives in this apartment building, and they've organized themselves so that every Saturday evening they get together in the lounge area for a potluck and card games. And some of our People—Kyra being one—are extremely gifted in the arts or diligent volunteers in the community."

"What about us? Why would you say we aren't successful?"

"Well, I was just thinking about how many evenings I go home tired and just pull out a frozen dinner. I go to the gym and to church, but sometimes I just think I'm on a treadmill no matter where I am. I used to paint, ride horses, have friends over. Now I just work and worry about everyone else's problems."

"I can see you are definitely ready for a new assignment," Barbara said. "I hope this will prove interesting for you. I don't really care which People you invite to participate in it, as long as they say they're interested. The two you mentioned might be fine. And don't forget, I want them to be included in the discussion phase when you finish the visits too. Their perspectives on what you've seen at the three places will be invaluable."

I was flattered to be asked to work on the project, and I told Barbara so. She handed me a stack of materials she wanted me to look over, along with a list of the three sites I was to visit and names of contacts at each site.

"The entire project should be completed in six weeks," she told me. That sounded like a short time for such a big project, but I wasn't surprised; that's often how these statewide grants work.

I'd heard of all three sites she'd included, but didn't know a lot about the organization of any of them. She listed the Creative Center, Hopedale Village, and the Streetside Café and Bakery. This was a big challenge, but I was eager to learn more about places with such enticing names.

"You might want to try to get out to one of the sites this week, if possible," Barbara told me. "Then schedule the other two visits for the following weeks, leaving the final three weeks to do your planning meetings and to write up the proposal. You can assign a bit more of your routine work to the interns, now that they've been here a while and know what's going on."

After our meeting I went to my office and called Hopedale Village, thinking it might be the logical choice for a first visit. The administrative office assistant there efficiently arranged for our tour on Friday, and I breathed a sigh of relief. My schedule for Friday had been light, and so I only needed to reschedule three visits. Darwin and Kyra could both accompany me on the trip, so I didn't need to reschedule their visits. I would just call them to make sure they'd be able to go.

Wednesday night came quickly that week, and this time it was *me* telling *Mel* all about my assignment. He'd come to my place before his class and I'd managed to cook dinner, a simple hot dish my mother always made for guests. It seemed like the sort of thing Mel would enjoy. When I was out that afternoon, I'd stopped at a roadside stand and bought a home-baked pie and a loaf of wheat bread. I wouldn't confess the truth about them, unless asked. I wasn't about to reveal my poorly developed cooking skills.

Earlier that afternoon I'd found time to read most of the materials Barbara had given me. The more I read, the more excited I became. The Creative Center was a renovated Victorian house in Akron, about an hour's drive north of Hilldale. A woman had left her estate to the mental-health board there in memory of her granddaughter, who had committed suicide as a young adult, the result of having severe, but undiagnosed, depression.

A not-for-profit agency had been formed, and they'd solicited volunteers from the university and a local arts associations to staff a drop-in center that included a ceramics studio, a large classroom that could also be used as a lecture hall or meeting room, a library, and a computer lab that included online services. A "quiet room" in the third-floor loft was furnished with desks, comfortable chairs, and plenty of pens, markers, notebooks, and even two notebook computers to stimulate poetry and journal writing.

"This is a far cry from the quiet rooms at the old state institutions," I thought, remembering the padded cells of yesteryear.

The Center was open to anyone in the community, but it was those in recovery who planned the programs and kept the place humming.

Streetside Café was a lunchroom in East Liverpool, along the Ohio River. It was described as a consumer-operated business that served soup-and-sandwich lunches to the public. Funded in part by workforce development grants, it was a training site for displaced workers getting ready to reenter the workforce. Some people with mental-health diagnoses worked there for months, or even years—whatever was best for them. Besides the luncheon offerings, the café housed a popular bakery that boasted the "Biggest & Best Oatmeal Cookies in the Nation."

Hopedale Village was the one project I was sure would interest Mel. I was setting the table but couldn't wait to start our dinner conversation.

"Hopedale Village is a thirty-acre farm that's been turned into an intentional community," I told him. "Most of the thirty residents are disabled in some way, either physically or mentally. About half of them are diagnosed with psychiatric disorders. The residents and a staff of eight grow organic fruits and vegetables and operate a roadside stand during the summer.

"And listen to this," I said to him, reading from the brochure. "In the winter they weave rag rugs and create costumes for a local theater company as well as offering for sale unique, one-of-a-kind wearables from donated clothing. The village also has a popular riding stable and a small sheep ranch."

"I know the place," he told me enthusiastically. "They grow garlic and I met the farm manager, Nate, at one of the garlic festivals. When I heard about them, I couldn't help thinking about Darwin. We talked quite a while about the whole operation there.

"What impresses me most, besides the success of that farm, is their holistic approach. I stopped in there one day on my way out to the Machinery Roundup in Westville. People working there were all so involved and knowledge-able. Very impressive. I ended up designing a piece of appropriate technology for one of the residents, who needed an adaptation so he could get his wheelchair onto the tractor. It turned out he liked the thing so much and it worked so well that he started his own lawn service and left."

"I thought you'd like Hopedale Village," I told Mel, "but I had no idea you'd actually been there." He looked at me sagely across the table and said, "There's a lot you don't know about me."

If only there had been more time for us to talk. Already it was time for Mel to get to his class. After a quick cleanup, my evening would be spent reading some more of Barbara's materials. It would be great to see Hopedale Village on Friday.

"Stop in after your class for coffee," I urged Mel.

"Sure. Of course."

As I watched the Dakota pull away, I thought about Rhonda's recent counsel and her "baptism." Maybe I was embarking on a new life already. At least I was feeling more hopeful than I had a few weeks back. The best thing though was seeing Mel every week. Just talking about things with someone who listened and seemed to care about me made such a difference.

But I noticed it was harder to keep my life in neat compartments.

Although I was looking forward to Friday and the visit to Hopedale, Thursday turned out to be interesting too. Kyra called the agency in the morning and asked if I could take her to the Shrine of St. Dymphna. She was already on my day's schedule, and I told her that would certainly be possible but suggested we move her appointment to the end of the day to give us more time. I believed in trying to be agreeable whenever I could. It had been a long time since I'd visited the old saint myself, and I was glad for the chance to see her again.

Kyra looked great when I picked her up. She'd brushed her black hair back and tied it with a thick scrunchie. Her earrings were silver and turquoise and looked expensive. When I commented, she said she'd found them at a thrift store—definitely a "find"! With her long skirt, sweater, shawl, and moccasins, she looked every bit the artist she was, and I told her so.

"I just kept thinking about St. Dymphna," she said. "I know it's silly of me to ask to go to the mental hospital, but this time it's to pray, not to be locked up."

I smiled at Kyra's comment. I hadn't been on the "campus" of Behavioral Health Center for months—that was its name in our new and enlightened era, but vestiges of the state hospital still remained. It had gone through several evolutions of both name and treatment modalities. But for most of us it was still "the state hospital."

The Shrine of St. Dymphna, patroness of those with mental and nervous disorders, was not well known, but many mental asylums had such shrines years ago. Dymphna's shrine was still kept up, and former patients sometimes visited there and found great solace. The days of praying at shrines are long gone for most people, but St. Dymphna had caught Kyra's attention.

State hospitals had once been asylums—truly asylums, that is, places of safety and refuge—for people with mental illness or other kinds of disabilities. The one we were going to visit had once housed more than three thousand people. They lived in eight "cottages." These large, lovely brick buildings had huge porches and well-maintained grounds. One of the early administrators had planted hundreds of species of plants and trees and had added fountains to the grounds. Both Catholic and Protestant chapels had been built for the patients.

They say an elaborate underground tunnel system used to connect the buildings. A farm on the huge tract where the hospital sat provided food for the entire complex. Little of this remained. Many of the buildings had been condemned and torn down.

Although they were created to provide humane treatment and shelter to those who came to them, through the years abuses occurred at the "asylums for the insane," as they were called. No one will ever know how many were "committed" who didn't need to be there. I glanced over at Kyra beside me in my car and felt grateful she had only spent a few days there in the past months.

During World War II, when conscientious objectors were assigned to work in the grossly understaffed hospitals, the true condition of the hospitals and the abuses of those who lived there came to light. In the years following the war, many reforms were made to the entire system, leading to what is now the community mental-health system in which I work.

Kyra was content to look out the window at the dull November landscape, and I felt grateful that this talented, artistic—though at times confused—woman didn't have to live her life in a locked hospital ward or work ten-hour days in the laundry room of an institution. I looked side-wise at her as I drove and asked, "Kyra, what can you tell me about St. Dymphna? I confess, I don't know much."

"She's our patron saint, you know. My grandmother had a picture of her in a book. She was a great woman. Gave me cookies with big raisins and let me sort through her button box." I knew she was talking about her grand-mother, not the saint, although maybe that grandmother was also a saint.

"I been to St. Dymphna lots," she said, getting back on track. "The old priest there—what's his name? He told me the whole story. Dymphna was an Irish princess whose mother died and then her pagan father tried to marry his own daughter. That is so awful! The priest and her ran away to Belgium but the soldiers caught up with them and killed them—cut off their heads." We shuddered.

"The village people built a church in her honor. Then the word spread and people started coming there to pray. People were healed. The town became famous because of all the miracles."

"That was back in the seventh century, in Gheel, Belgium," I said, seizing the teachable moment. "Even back then people had psychiatric illnesses. I've heard that today the city of Gheel is known for the compassion the townspeople have for the pilgrims who come there."

Kyra pulled a small, very worn envelope from the pocket in her skirt. "Here she is," she said, holding out a picture. I took a quick look as I kept driving. The saint in the picture looked calm. She carried a book in one hand and something that seemed like a sword in the other. On her head was a crown, and her robes swirled around her feet.

I turned the car into the winding lane of the hospital grounds. Only a few patients lived there—less than two hundred. Most came only for a short stay and then went back to the community, to receive services like ours, sometimes to their homes and families, and unfortunately, sometimes to a crude shelter under a bridge or, in a rural areas, a shack in the woods or a dilapidated trailer on a relative's farm. The asylums are gone, but the system that has replaced them is far from perfect. "Yes, Dr. Larch, apartheid still exists," I thought.

Kyra and I shivered as we got out of the car. It was getting colder, and we leaned into the wind as we made our way to the chapel. A light was shining at the entrance and the heavy, carved, wooden doors were unlocked. We stepped into the chapel and looked up. Our saint smiled on us with a faint, calm reassurance.

I sat in the first pew and Kyra fell heavily on the kneeling bench in front of St. Dymphna, stretching her cast-covered leg sidewise. I could hear her breathing slow down as she knelt, her skirt swirling behind her and her shawl cascading over her shoulders. I wondered what she was thinking, what she was praying. Perhaps not words, but a simple reaching of the heart for healing.

I picked up a leaflet someone had left on the pew and read once again the story of the saint. "Every home in Gheel is proud to welcome to its inmost family circle such patients as are ready to return to the environment of family life," the blue print on the pamphlet said.

"Generations of experience have given the people of Gheel an intimate and tender skill in dealing with their charges, and their remarkable spirit of charity and Christ like love for these afflicted members of society gives our modern-day world, so prone to put its whole reliance on science and to forget the principle of true Christian charity, a lesson the practice of which would do much to restore certain types of mentally afflicted individuals to an almost normal outlook on life."

The language was out of date, and yet the ideas were still viable, to my mind. Science can help. But it can go only so far.

I looked again at St. Dymphna and back to Kyra, bowed there before her. I thought of a question Rhonda had asked me once. We were talking about my work and my anger and frustration about the limitations and over-whelming problems of my People. She'd asked, "What would make a difference for your People?"

Just then an elderly man opened the door and paused briefly when he saw us. He wore a clerical collar under a worn tweed jacket. He stuffed a rosary into his pocket and greeted us as walked over.

"Ah, you've come t' pray t' Dymphna," he said with good humor. I nodded and Kyra quickly rose to her feet.

"Don't let me interrupt," he said. "I'm Father Gershten." I felt amused with the suggestion of Irish brogue mixed into the Ohio idiom.

"Here, come, let us pray together." Father Gershten walked over to us, and I noticed the gray jogging shoes and snagged, polyester dress slacks. He reached out to me and Kyra and placed one arm on each of our shoulders. I expected a formal high-church prayer, but instead he spoke simply and conversationally. Instead of St. Dymphna, he addressed "God, our Father and Creator."

I appreciated his simple gesture, which seemed to suggest an answer for the question Rhonda had asked, the question still rumbling around in my mind: What would make a difference? One thing I was sure of, it would be something beyond programs, services, and medications. Perhaps a saint, a prayer.

15

AFTER WORK I DROVE the ten miles to the rail trail parking lot, where Mel was waiting for me in the Dakota. He had a backpack slung over his shoulder and carried binoculars and a field guide.

"Do you have a warm jacket?" he asked.

"I remembered this time," I said, pulling a coat and scarf from the back seat and exchanging my loafers for hiking boots. The landscape was losing its luster but there were still trees with a smattering of colored leaves, their shine heightened by the late-afternoon sun.

"This won't be a long hike, but enough time to see any lingering migrating birds and to be together without interruption," Mel said.

Again I felt a twinge of guilt when I thought about how Darwin would feel if he learned of our meeting. He would have enjoyed a hike too, I was fairly certain of that.

"Who's doing the milking for you?" I asked. My memories served me well and I was already tuned in again to the rhythms of farm life.

"Paulie and a couple of his boys will come over tonight. I'm sure glad I can get away once in a while. Of course I didn't have much peace about what I was running off for."

"Oh, they're teasing you, are they?" I interjected with a smile.

"Yeah. They know about the classes though, so they weren't too hard on me."

The colors shone, even in that cold, gray time of year.

The subtle blues and greens of evergreens were visible in the brush and reflected in the standing water of the marsh, which was edged with cattails and full of water plants. Wood ducks bobbed on the calm surface and light bounced off their colorful feathers. A desire to paint rose inside me.

Mel said he'd come there more than once for birding. He called this wetland "the swamp." It covered acres and, like a giant earth-sponge, held moisture and released it as needed into the atmosphere. Winding roads made their way through the swamp unless the water got too high. The best way to see it though, if you wanted to stay dry, was to take the trail.

We came to a part that was waiting for construction to make it useful for recreation. An old cement bridge with vines hanging over it stood near the place where we left our vehicles. It was a reminder that trains once passed that way, taking lumber out and bringing coal in.

We walked in silence, listening to our own footsteps, and I recognized the wonder of finding another human being whose footfalls matched my own. It was such a small thing, just our steps together on this land where we'd both grown up. And yet there was something miraculous about our being there and being together like that.

I pulled my jacket closer and shivered. Mel squeezed my hand, trying to warm me up. "There is an amazing diversity of wildlife in this area," he told me. "Whitetail deer and Canada geese, of course. But even coyote. And beaver. The beavers were missing from the ecosystem here for 150 years, but have now returned. Their dam building has created even more wetland habitats for other animals."

"Look at that bird. What is it?" I asked pointing to a long-legged creature with a huge, prehistoric-looking beak.

"That's a great blue heron," Mel said. "They have a

wing span of over seven feet when they're airborne, and they glide on the air currents. They live high in the trees, which is why we're seeing one here. We'll have to come back in the spring and watch their mating behavior. The heron lover is a gentleman all the way, bowing to the lady, his bill snapping, feathers all ruffled in excitement."

Mel's eyes sparkled as he acted out the blue heron's antics. "And best of all, I'll fly to you with a twig offering." He reached down and handed me a small stick from the ground. "When you accept this, you'll know I'm for keeps—repairing the nest and keeping the home fires burning, so to speak."

I accepted the twig and put it in my pocket. It would end up on my windowsill, a reminder of an afternoon I would not want to forget. "Well, that sounds good," I said. "I could use some help around the house." I squeezed his hand and felt warmer.

I was beginning to wish Mel would be more up front and talkative about us and our relationship. Maybe we really were engaging in our own mating dance. Every time we got close, one of us pulled away. He was almost secretive sometimes, despite his genuine sense of humor and good-natured banter. And just when he seemed ready to be close, I'd have a failure of nerve and retreat.

A sign posted at the overlook read "Do Something Wild!" It was advertising the nature conservancy, suggesting we contribute to the cause. Although I'd once spent hours outdoors, as I'd grown older I'd drifted further and further into the sea of humanity. Coming to the marsh was good for me. I felt grounded. Maybe I did need to do something wild—take a hike instead of shopping or working out at the health club. If Mel had ideas about what it meant to "do something wild," he didn't let on. A few minutes later I knew otherwise.

"Let's stop and rest. Come here. We'll sit over here."
Mel led me to the side of the trail and held back a few
branches. I followed him to a level spot where the fallen
leaves of maples and oaks mixed with beech and ash.
There they made a soft bed under our feet. Mel opened the
backpack and took out a picnic blanket. He spread it
gracefully in front of us, then brought out sandwiches and
a bottle of grape juice. He invited me to sit with him on the
blanket. I thought of Holy Communion as I ate the bread
and drank the juice. It might have been another humble
ritual, but I didn't have the imaginative banter to make it
work as Rhonda did that day at the springhouse.

As we ate, in the stillness of the woods I heard a
strange sound. Mel put his hand on my sleeve and signaled
for me to listen. We turned our heads in unison toward the
sound and saw a strong, young buck standing just a few
yards away, looking at us. We held his gaze, not flinching,
for fear of scaring him. He snorted twice and was gone,
bounding off through the woods.

"Did you see that?" Mel exclaimed, although he knew
I had.

We finished the sandwiches and stashed our trash in
the backpack. Mel lay back on the blanket and looked up
through the bare branches to the late-afternoon sky.

"What are you thinking," I asked him.

"Oh, nothing, I guess."

"Come on, what?

Mel reached for me and gently pulled me down beside
him, saying nothing. He placed my head on his arm with
one hand, and gathered me to himself with the other. We
kissed as if we each held all the life we'd ever need or want.
I wanted him as if there were not days and weeks ahead
when we would move through all the predictable stages
that bring two people to what was happening. Now, in

deference to us, time stood still. Perhaps nature knew the truth about our coming together. The wind stirred and a few red leaves fluttered down, showering us with a benediction.

And then, from the shelter of a stand of blooming goldenrod flanked by a tangle of multiflora rose bramble, we heard the buck snorting again, furiously. It was as if he wanted, in this moment, to be part of what was ours alone. We held our breath, and it seemed only one breath. The buck snorted over and over and pawed the leaves. We heard the rustle of his desire in the stillness of our coming together. "Sh-h-h-h! This is for us."

Mel's lively eyes gathered himself into my spirit. I let myself be drawn into the warmth of what we were being given—a spirit bond nothing in heaven or on earth will ever break.

We stayed there on the floor of the forest and held one another for a long time, trying to assuage all the moments of loneliness that lay piled between us, numberless as the drifting leaves. And we knew, no matter what happened now, our spirits would be forever entangled in one another and in the heart of the earth, which brought our love to life.

"This is for us," he said. "This is for us."

"It's grace." I said. "Grace."

℮

We finally made our way back to the trailhead, listening to the soft plodding of our steps along the path.

"Mel?"

"Yeah?"

"I wish . . ., I hope . . ."

Mel squeezed my hand. "Me too, Angie. I had to keep thinkin' back there: 'do not stir up, nor awaken love, until it pleases.'"

"What?"

"It's from Solomon's Song. The Bible. Chapter 8. Verse 4. Read it sometime."

"Well, okay. I think I know what you mean."

After that our conversation continued on. Anyone listening would not have detected a difference, but I knew we were growing closer. We'd made an unspoken covenant that we would have a future together, somehow, in the right season.

Now we wanted to share our deepest thoughts, our passions, and our disappointments. Our relationship was becoming as surefooted as our steps on the solid, cinder-covered path of the abandoned rail trail. Mel and I wrapped our arms behind one another's waists and walked easily in step as we talked.

It may have been our talk of the swamp and of the natural world that brought to mind something important Mel wanted me to know. "Every time I come here to the swamp," Mel began, letting his eyes rest on the water plants beyond the trail, "I think of the rice paddies of Laos."

"You love that place, don't you?" I asked. Now I could hear his love for the landscape, just as I could hear his love for me, in every syllable he spoke.

"I just can't forget the gardens, the rice fields, the water buffalo, and the peaceful way of life—the way it used to be for the people in my village. It hurts to think that some of those places are off-limits now. Posted. Not to protect wildlife, but to protect the villagers."

"What do you mean, posted to protect the villagers?"

Mel told me that some of the gardens where the Lao people in his village grew peppers and the other garden plants they depended on for food, along with many of the rice paddies, were now considered danger zones. The "crops" planted there have a deadly yield, not at all the increased production he'd worked for as a community developer.

"A crop of bomblets, cluster bombs—they call them 'bombies' over there—is gradually working its way up from the soil into the open air," Mel said. "When they get close to the surface, they can maim or kill an innocent farmer or even a child whose curiosity causes him to pick up the small ordnance, thinking it might be a toy or a useful object."

I couldn't believe what I was hearing. I may have read about this in a news article after the death of Lady Diana, who was concerned about those cluster bombs, but I'd never considered the horrific consequences.

"I left the small village where I worked for three years, in the Xieng Khouang province. I'd been there helping people plant gardens and improve their livestock and bringing in some technology to make their farming easier, all the while not creating a dependency on foreign aid. It was hard work, but I left feeling we'd really made their lives better.

"We now know that, soon after, the United States military began secretly bombing Laos. I guess it was their way of showing support for the Royal Lao government, which was committed to our side. And we were helping them destroy the communist regime that was taking hold there. Laos was a training ground for troops that were moving into Vietnam.

"These cluster bombs were about the size of a tennis ball or a baseball. They were filled with small fragments of metal designed to injure and maim, and specifically designed *not* to harm equipment, only people."

I shivered.

"I heard a program where they talked about them and showed some one time," Mel continued. "It was being toured around by the Mennonite Central Committee. They wanted us to know what the cluster bombs were like because they are trying to raise funds to assist with cleanup."

"How can they be cleaned up if they're as dangerous as you say?" I asked.

"It isn't easy. A lot of work is still being done on it, all these years later. In the meantime, once-valuable agricultural land is 'posted.'"

"So, how many bombies would there be in a village, for instance?"

"We really have no idea about individual bomblets. We do know that from 1964 to 1973, our government engaged in the heaviest air bombing ever seen in the world. During that time there were 580,300 bombing missions flown and six million tons of bombs dropped on a land that had a population of about three million at the time of the war.

"That means there was a strike every eight minutes for nine years. It's been calculated our government dropped two tons of bombs per capita. Many of these bombs never exploded and they still desecrate the land, effectively taking it out of production for probably decades."

"What did the people in your village do?" I asked.

"For a time, many of them fled to Vientiane, the capital city of Laos, where it was relatively safe. But when the war ended, many of them returned to the countryside. Everywhere they went, they heard more news about the dangers of the bombies. Through the years, many people— adults and children—lost their lives as they tried to grow food in their own gardens. There's no other way to support themselves but to farm."

"Won't the bombies eventually wear out and not be a danger to people, as time goes on?"

"Unfortunately, sometimes bombies lie buried in the

ground for many years. Gradually they rise to the surface or are uncovered during cultivation of the land. I went back to Laos a couple of years after the war officially ended. I was a Mennonite representative on a team trying to find a solution. Mennonites, because we're pacifists and against war, are trusted. People in other countries know of our interest in providing basic food, shelter, and technology to people around the world. They call it humanitarian aid, but for us, it is taken there in the name of Christ.

"During my visit, I was with a Mines Advisory Council, a British group that was working to find a way to clear the land so the people could return and rebuild their villages and plant their gardens again. But the problem was—still is—so widespread. There are really no easy solutions."

"I can see how awful that must be for you, having lived in that very place." I squeezed Mel's middle to let him know I felt his sadness.

"Almost every village we visited," he continued, "had a terrible story to tell us about someone who died while planting their rice paddy, or who had accidentally hit one with their hoe, causing it to explode. Many farmers and even children have lost an arm or a leg or have been blinded. Children sometimes mistake the bombies for a toy, or a ball. And the results are devastating.

"What hurts me the most is that almost no one is even aware of this. It's old news for the media, but the legacy of our actions lives on and affects the daily lives of so many people. Yet the Lao farmers have no choice but to work their land, because they have to feed their families. The most anyone has been able to do is to try to educate people about the dangers of the bombies. A few efforts have been made to find a way to detect and detonate the bombies, but it's an overwhelming task.

"For these simple farmers, there's no other way to

support yourself if you live in that area. They will farm some of that land. It's about as rural as it gets out there. All these years have gone by and no one seems to remember or care. I still think about the man who shook his head sadly and said to me, 'The Americans have money to come over here and look for the bones of soldiers, but they don't want to help us look for bombs.' I just can't get that out of my mind. I think about it when I'm out plowing my own fields and when I'm harvesting. When a rock is thrown up while I'm cultivating the corn, I look at it sometimes and think, 'What if this was a bombie?'

"I wonder what my friends in the village are doing, if there are bombies in the fields we worked in together when I was there helping them develop their community. I haven't had word from them for a long time. What must they think of those of us who worked alongside them developing their land, only to learn that our government dumped tons of bombs on them less than a year later?"

I let the silence lay between us. There was nothing I could say. And now we shared this pain that had once been his to carry alone. We had both been wounded by our life's experiences; I was finding out just how much. And our earth had been wounded too.

We had been standing for some time, leaning against the tailgate of the Dakota, knowing we would go our separate ways. Mel would be late for his class if he didn't leave soon. I would go home and wait for him to stop afterward. I reached up and put my arms around him, holding him tight and kissing him deeply, returning the energy I'd borrowed. Our spirits had joined in love, and the expanse of our love was becoming a home—a home-place. Yet I knew it was also so much more. I knew it reached into the earth and spread across the globe.

16

I DECIDED TO SORT through the art supplies I'd bought at the yard sale, so I retrieved the canvases from the trunk of my car, and the train case, which was still just inside the back door.

Years ago I'd been so passionate about art that I'd almost chosen it as my college major. But I settled on social work, which seemed more practical. Maybe it was in deference to my social-activist mom, who pushed me toward the service ethic that she thought suited me. My family tended to embody the kind of practicality and outer-directed enterprise you often find in rural communities. These were strong, pragmatic people, whose ancestors came in covered wagons and understood the meaning of a good day's work.

So, along the way I'd pushed my art aside for things that seemed to have more value, things like helping and taking care of other people. I felt a kinship with the mother of that woman at the yard sale, and I thought I understood why she might have stopped painting.

The canvases were mostly untouched and ready to use. A couple had false starts on them—a rough sketch or a few dabs of paint. One was painted, but seemed somehow unfinished. I couldn't decide what it needed. Maybe just more texture and depth that could be brought out by adding layers of paint.

"This must be the picture she said I might finish," I thought as I examined it. It was one I could identify with: an old farmhouse with a rambling porch. In the foreground were several geese with their necks outstretched, as if they were running from something.

"What are you running from?" I asked them. I could almost see a young girl, pigtails flying, running just beyond the edge of the picture. "Maybe that was you, afraid or unable to paint yourself into the picture. Was this your home, your homeplace?"

I was amused by my discussion with the picture and the imagination that had so easily carried me away. I propped the canvas against the wall on a narrow table in my kitchen and studied it. Then I opened the train case and began sorting the supplies into piles on a tray.

I dabbed fresh paint on much of the surface of the canvas, carefully avoiding the geese and the section to the right of them. I was glad the yard-sale woman had given her blessing to the possibility of adding my own embellishments.

There was a knock at the door, and I realized I'd lost all track of time and had completely forgotten dinner. It was Rhonda.

"Angie, so sorry I didn't call. I was in town this afternoon for a meeting that ran late and thought I'd stop by and see what's new."

"Well, nothing much, I guess. Come on in."

Rhonda was surprised when she saw the canvas and smelled the fresh paint. "What do you mean, 'nothing much'? This looks pretty big to me! Looks like you're taking my advice already. "

I told her about the yard sale and the woman's comment. Rhonda sat down in front of the picture and studied it.

"What a picture of home!" she exclaimed. "It reminds me of a place I want to live. A long, dirt lane, an old white house. It just draws me into it somehow."

"I know," I said. "When I saw this, I started imagining all kinds of things." I didn't tell her the house reminded me of Mel's place or that I'd imagined painting myself into the picture, herding the geese.

"I guess we carry with us this longing for home," Rhonda said. She was getting spiritual on me again, as she did so easily.

"I know what you mean. I felt like that the day I found Mel's place. There was something about that farm that just made me feel as if I were coming home."

Rhonda looked at me strangely and I realized I'd revealed the very thing I was trying to hide. I still hadn't told anyone about the day I'd gone to see Darwin there. "You've been to his place?" she asked. Her eyes widened with surprise.

"Well, yes. I did go one time," I confessed.

"Things are moving faster than I thought," she said, giving me a long look.

My silence revealed my reticence to talk about Mel just then. I felt a flush rise to my cheeks when I thought of the day before, which now seemed much longer ago than the twenty hours it had actually been. If my friend noticed, she didn't say.

Rhonda, maybe sensing my constraint, continued with the more spiritual tone. "I think this longing for home isn't always for a real place as much as for something more intangible. Think of all those old Gospel hymns about heaven. I'm not so sure this heaven they sing about might not be something inside of us, instead of a far-off city with golden streets."

"What do you mean?" I asked.

"I don't know exactly, but I think sometimes we close ourselves off from the very things inside of us that could awaken us. Heaven could shine right inside our own souls. Maybe those old songs are a form of poetry that expresses this longing we all have."

"Just like this picture does for me," I mused. "Hey, would you like to share a frozen pizza? I haven't eaten yet. I was so busy dabbing paint, I forgot."

"Well, sure. I haven't eaten either. Dale works late tonight, and I was planning to just eat a salad at home."

I got the box from my freezer and turned on the oven, then I poured a goblet of Chardonnay for each of us. I told Rhonda about the hike with Mel, skipping the parts that were too beautiful for words. Some things are meant to be told; other things are pictures we store in our minds to guide us on the journey. She would know that, I'm sure.

"Things founded clean on their own shapes, water and ground in the extremity." Again stray lines of the Seamus Heaney poem pushed their way into my consciousness.

Rhonda and I went on talking into the evening. Our friendship was weaving us together, and I saw pictures forming in my imagination, pictures I could paint: a river, a path, a home where I wanted to live.

ৼ

After Rhonda left, I soaked in a bath scented with oil of lavender. I'd bought this essential oil, as the shop clerk called it, because she told me it was calming and induced relaxation. Even though it was late, I felt keyed up and needed to unwind. I was thankful tomorrow was Saturday and I could sleep in.

But the lavender had the opposite effect on me. As scents sometimes do, it brought back unwanted and long-buried memories. I wrapped myself in a white bath sheet and quickly found my threadbare pajamas.

The experience of dabbing paint on the canvas and the scent of lavender mingled in my imagination, as other amalgams of experience had recently. A picture I had painted years ago appeared unbidden in my mind's eye. It too was an oil. During a break after college, before we entered graduate school, several of us had escaped the chaotic university scene for a bicycle trip in Europe. We rode through Italy and France, packing our ten-speed bikes onto the train at times. We stayed in youth hostels and anywhere we could find cheap lodging.

I'd taken hundreds of photos that summer in the landscape where Van Gogh had spent so many hours. Maybe I knew in years to come I'd need the inspiration of his creative spirit, coupled as it was with a disturbed mind. In my search for perfect composition I'd taken several gorgeous shots of the lavender fields of Provence. The following semester I enrolled in a landscape painting class, and my photos and memories of that trip became my class project.

During those weeks in France I fell in love with Reid. We had started the trip merely as friends, but ended it as lovers. The days of riding, the evenings of wine and music, and the beauty of the pastoral countryside had drawn us to each other and sealed our hope for a future together. We parted with a promise ringing in our ears. But first I would enter graduate school, and Reid would have to keep another promise: He'd enlisted for a tour of duty in Vietnam that was to begin immediately after our return.

These memories prompted an overwhelming impulse to find *Lavender in Provence,* a painting from one of those photographs. The need outweighed any thoughts about the lateness of the hour. Fueled by a rush of adrenaline, I began to search storage closets, shelves in my garage, and even the furnace room. All to no avail. Somewhere, I knew, there was a painting hidden away in a dark place. I searched as though possessed, frantic. The Provence hillsides had reminded me of places in Ohio where there were still small farms and rolling hills dotted with cattle and sheep, gardens and fields. I loved that landscape as I loved my own.

When I finally found the picture, it was well past midnight. I'd backed my car out of the garage, pulled down the trap door from the ceiling, and climbed the stairs to the attic. The unframed canvas was wrapped in a garbage bag covered with dust. I dropped the bag onto the garage floor and carefully carried its contents into the house. Miraculously, it hadn't been damaged by the changing temperatures, and it looked just as I remembered.

I propped the painting against the fireplace, opposite the sofa. I was still cold from being in the unheated garage dressed only in my pajamas, so I gathered myself into my grandmother's wool comforter.

I watched the shadows of the room cast themselves onto my picture. The warm light from my table lamp spilled over my created work and the deep-purple, periwinkle, and blue-green hues softened to a watery impressionistic presence. I gazed with respect and admiration on the work of my own hands, created years ago. And then I was crying.

I cried with the uncontrollable sobs of one who is heartbroken for the first time. As my heart opened to its bottom, to the very bottom of that well of pain and disappointment, I traveled to the core of the insatiable longings, deep hunger, and dark emptiness of all I'd lost. I felt the depths of all that could never be returned to me, no matter how long I lived.

I sat wrapped in the comforter, barely conscious, and sobbed, gathering tissues from the coffee table until I could cry no longer. I wept for everything in my life that was wrong. And then for every sorrow of my life: the loss of my childhood faith, the loss of Reid, the harsh ending of my marriage to Don. I cried for the way Darwin and others I served had been rejected, for the cruelty of illnesses that twist brain synapses and alter the minds of my People, leaving them with so few choices. I cried for the tragedy of Mel and Loretta's short life together. I cried for the desecration of the landscape in Laos and for the deaths of innocent children because of the bombies. I cried for the policies and doctrines that the best self knows are wrong. And for the hard journey it becomes when we set out to make the wrongs right and to work for justice.

"Let justice roll down like waters," Rhonda had said. Is the water our tears?

My mind went numb after that. In the lateness of the hour, I reabsorbed the warmth that gathered around me inside the old comforter. I heard a soft voice that I seemed to recognize, but that I could not identify. "Are you warm? Do you feel warm now?"

There in my cocoon, it was as if feeling warm—such a common, simple thing—was a precursor for my healing, and not to be overlooked. So I stayed wrapped in this warmth of my own making. It reflected itself back into me, into the core of my being, into my soul, which finally began to heal.

17

THE BARN DOOR was heavier than I'd expected. I was looking for Mel, who seemed nowhere to be found that Saturday afternoon. I'd once again easily found my way to the homeplace. A pungent smell wafted from inside the barn. I spied Darwin, ski cap pulled low over his eyebrows, scooping manure out of the barn with the loader, a cigarette dangling from his lips. He was smiling, having fun, but I couldn't imagine how he could enjoy such a smelly job. The sun was shining and the sky was blue. When I looked up, it was a pretty picture framed by the open barn doors.

Mel knew I was coming to pick up Darwin. Where was he anyway? I'd half expected him to be waiting for me in the house, but that was probably unrealistic when there was plenty to do outside. Maybe he was up on the barn floor, working on a piece of equipment.

I'd surprised him there last week one evening. In the light of a shaft of late-afternoon sunlight slanting through a gap in the siding, I'd found Mel lying in the haymow holding a book up into the light. Tools lay strewn across the floor below. The grease gun rested on a feed sack. Dust hung thick on a sunbeam and showered him, making his face sparkle.

"Mel?" I'd hollered.

"Oh!" He'd leapt up with a start and leaned on one

elbow, peering down at me. "I'm taking a short break," he said. I couldn't help noticing a guilty look on his face.

"That's okay. You need one. Looks like you're making progress," I said, gesturing to the corn picker and the pieces lying on the floor. I leaned against an orange gravity flow wagon and watched him slide down the bales to the worn planks of the barn floor. His jeans were tight enough to make me notice, his hair the color of the straw in the other mow.

"Gary Snyder, hmm," I'd said, reaching for the poetry book. He took it quickly back and stuffed it in an inner pocket of his barn coat, where it bulged slightly.

"You like him?" I asked curiously.

"Well, in a way, I guess. But I could do without all that Buddhist crap," he said ungraciously.

Mel was certainly candid. Sometimes his broad-mindedness impressed me, like when he talked about the cluster bombs. Other times he reverted to some inborn narrow-mindedness that probably shouldn't surprise me, given his upbringing.

ॐ

Now a week later, I trudged again up the barn hill to the upper barn floor, hoping he'd be somewhere nearby.

"What a great invention the bank barn is," Mel had once explained to me. "The sloping ground heaped up to the second story is a wide lane, angled just right for rigging ropes and pulleys to drag the hay in, the way they used to before machinery took over."

I checked inside—both the haymow and the straw mow. The siding had been repaired but Mel wasn't inside. Finally I heard the John Deere coming in from the field. Mel was standing up, off the tractor seat. My heart lurched forward to greet him as he waved, but my feet stayed where they were. Buster barked and rushed for me. His fur was spotted with patches of manure, and I pulled back.

"Hey! It's too nice a day for that!" I shouted over the roar. Mel throttled the tractor and it rolled to a stop.

"You know what they say, don't you?" Mel asked with a welcoming smile. Our conversation picked up as if the one several days earlier had never ended.

"No, what?" I asked. "Make hay while the sun shines?"

"Uh-uh. Not today. Haul shit till the barn's clean," he said irreverently, trying to upset me with his attempted profanity.

"Oh, so that's what I smell," I teased, holding my nose.

"I need to educate you, city girl. Here, climb up on this seat and I'll give you your first tractor-driving lesson."

"Not today. Maybe sometime when you're a little cleaner."

"Meet me down below," he yelled as he let out the clutch.

I headed for the barn cellar, where the cows lived. They were still "on pasture," as Mel would say. Grazing saves hay and silage and makes milk with more nutrients. At least that's what Mel believed. It also keeps manure-hauling to a minimum during the three warmer seasons.

"Let's go in the house for a little. I could use a cup of coffee."

On our way to the porch, Mel started to educate me on the benefits of manure. "Manure is holy," he said with a twinkle in his eye. I loved his easy talk about the farm, and I listened as much for the pleasure of hearing him talk as for what he was telling me. "It's a whole mixture of things. You start with some straw on the barn floor. The animals' urine and dung mix into the straw used for bedding. The livestock stirs the brew together with their hooves and tread it down. In the winter the hard manure pack on the floor insulates the animals from the cold and keeps the barn snug. In spring we clean the barn, spread the manure on the fields, and then plow it under."

Mel was always ready with a story. I thought of him romantically as a monk of sorts—maybe a Zen monk. He may not have been sure about Gary Snyder, but his farm oozed Zen. He wouldn't have seen it that way, of course; it was practicality and old-fashioned values that guided his plans for those forty-eight acres.

"It's farming that brought me back to Ohio," he told me as we lounged on the porch, holding our steaming coffee. "I had my questions about some of the Mennonite beliefs, just like a lot of the young people—especially back during Vietnam. Why should I stay where it's safe while my buddies were all being shipped out? I guess joining the Peace Corps was my way of rebelling while keeping the faith, but in my own way.

"When I came back, I knew I wanted to farm Dad's place using the old ways. There's a limit to what technology can do for a farmer. I look around, and all over the place guys are losing their shirts, buying bigger and bigger tractors and combines. I see guys going in debt to buy up farms and then they go belly up. Like Paulie says, 'Depreciation don't pay the bills.'

"I did a lot of reading about sustainable agriculture, partly for my work in Laos. You talk to the older farmers at church and you hear what works and what doesn't work. Anyway, it was an easy sell after my experiences in Southeast Asia. Small farmers growing rice and catching fish in the river. I saw how their lives were simple and good, the way many of my ancestors' lives were till modern agriculture took over.

"I was there to help *them*, but sometimes I thought I

was the one learning more. You can get too much cash tied up in machinery. You only need a certain amount of it to get the job done. Asians manage pretty well with a water buffalo and a crude plow, a few hand tools, the appropriate technology we were able to design for them."

"Those old ways, your people, the farmers in your church—what did they do?" I asked.

"Well, back in eighteenth-century Europe, the Anabaptist farmers developed this system of crop rotation that produced high yields but helped nature keep its balance. In fact, it was so successful it may have spawned the Industrial Revolution."

"How so?"

"Never underestimate the power of manure, is what I always say! The rich yields of these farms brought new wealth and the need for machinery to harvest and process the grain.

"In the old way, you have a four-year crop rotation. A field is planted only with corn every fourth year. After corn, the field is sowed in oats. After it's harvested, the stubble is plowed under. First we haul a few loads of manure, don't forget, and then wheat is sown. The wheat is seeded the following year with legume seeds: alfalfa or clover."

Mel said the word *alfalfa* with pleasure. I could hear it in his voice, almost reverence. I liked the lacy texture and the small, blue blossoms of alfalfa too, but Mel's respect was deeper. Alfalfa is part of the secret equation that a farmer like Mel would know.

Mel couldn't sit still long. He picked up a few twigs from the lawn and snapped them off in short lengths, laying out fields on the porch floor as he talked. I watched a patchwork quilt of sticks take shape and visualized the fields and crops in turn.

"Next thing you know, it's time to combine the wheat, and like a miracle, the wheat field turns into a hayfield."

Our eyes wandered across the lane to the distant green field, now striped dark with the brew from Mel's manure spreader.

"The next spring and summer we harvest several cuttings of hay, then the hayfield is pastured in the fall. It's during the winter—these short days coming at us now—that the old sod is plastered over with manure. That's what you're smelling. We say that's the smell of money." Mel laughed at the joke, obviously oft-repeated.

"Come spring, as soon as we can get into the fields, that hayfield will be planted again with corn, and the cycle starts over."

I began to look at the farms and the countryside in a new way after talking with Mel. And the "fresh country air" we sometimes mocked as we drove the back roads now had a new meaning for me. I thought about the red clover blossoms and blue alfalfa that filled the ditches. They are there because of farmers like Mel who spread their wealth.

"Farming is chemistry," Mel told me. "The formula is as precise as pharmacology. The healing grasses—legumes—convert free nitrogen from the air to the soil. Add ten to fifteen tons of manure per acre, and you double the nitrogen per ton. You can farm with hardly any fertilizer."

My dad would have approved of Mel, I think. He certainly would have appreciated this lesson more than I could. And he'd have added some of his own observations and probably peddled a couple of his products if he thought they would improve yields.

*

I leaned against the peeling porch post and ran my hand up and down, feeling the flakes sift under my fingers. Mel's farm talk chipped away at my social-work mentality. What he was doing seemed positive and healthy: feeding people, taking care of the land. In contrast, my frail attempts to provide support for troubled humans seemed daunting.

"What are you thinking, Angie? You seem so far away. Am I boring you?"

"No, not at all. It's just that what you do seems so wholesome and uplifting. I get so discouraged with my work sometimes. Endless problems and tangled human relationships. Systems that don't work like they're supposed to." I sighed as I breathed in the farm and barnyard smells, and brushed the paint chips from my palms onto the porch floor.

"Well, we have our problems too. Broken machinery, low milk prices, you name it. I guess it's more about what you focus on and where you put your mind."

At that moment, we heard the scream of a red-tailed hawk. We stood there together watching as he flew onto a bare branch of a tall, dead tree in the pasture.

"There she flies," he said with a touch of awe in his voice. "The hawk knows how to live. I'm glad she didn't die from West Nile virus last summer.

"A hawk will sit up in the top of a tree at the edge of the field. You see them up there looking out over a field like they're wise old women. And then they catch sight of a mole and down they go. Dinner. See big picture; zero in. Not a bad plan."

"I suppose so," I admitted.

"I don't know about you, but things are sure looking a lot better now that you've come along." Mel glanced my way with a soft look on his face, and I wanted a hug. But I didn't want to smell like the barn.

"I know," I said. "I guess our lives are a little bit like the life of the farm. Cycles of growing, fading, dying off, and resting. Getting rid of the shit, then starting all over again."

Mel grinned. I'd gotten him back with his own dirty word.

"We need to talk about Darwin. I'm not sure how he's taking all of this," I said, motioning to show I meant the connection between me and Mel.

"I know. I think he's caught on. I probably said too much about you the other day. He got sullen after I mentioned you a couple of times. Didn't say anything much though. I hate it that he's bothered."

"*You* hate it?" I said. I looked up at him and caught his eyes as they locked onto mine. "What about me? I could be in deep do-do, to phrase it more delicately."

"What do you mean?"

"I shouldn't have ever come out here that first weekend. We're supposed to keep strict boundaries between ourselves and Helping Hands clients. Socializing and weekend visits would be frowned on. In fact, it could be worse than that. People have been known to be severely disciplined, lose jobs, for something like this."

"But if you'd never come out here, we'd probably never have met."

"It's strange. I should feel bad, guilty even. But I don't. I'm mostly worried about Darwin's reaction. I guess my boss doesn't know anything about this. After all, she gave me the new assignment, didn't she?"

Just then Darwin came around the corner of the house, and I had an uneasy feeling he might have heard us talking about him. He walked past without looking at the two of us. We'd instinctively stepped apart, and I'd walked over to inspect the rhubarb—a useless gesture at that time of year. I moved toward the garlic, which showed signs of new shoots coming up.

I heard Mel offer Darwin a cup of coffee, and then the screen door slammed. I stayed there in the garden looking across the pasture toward the hawk still perched on the branch and thought of the canvases waiting to be painted with landscapes—hawks, gardens, and fields. I felt excited about getting started on Barbara's project. Most of all, I was starting to imagine a life that included Mel.

There were many things I'd never have to live through again because I'd made my peace with them, plowed them under where they'd nurture the new life of another season. I was blessed beyond belief and decided not to worry about Darwin too much. After all, everything happens for a reason, they say.

ℰ

"I keep thinking about something Rhonda talks about," I told Mel later when Darwin went back to the barn. "About being a compassionate presence. I guess in a way she's been that for me. You, too. When you find a friend who knows how to truly listen to your experiences and your feelings, it gives you this new kind of courage to keep going."

"I know. Makes a difference, doesn't it?"

"I felt so lost for a time there. And disconnected. Did I tell you about the art supplies I found at a garage sale?"

"No. Art supplies?"

I told Mel the whole story. About Reid, about putting the *Lavender in Provence* in the attic, and about the canvas that made me think of Mel's place as a home where people gather to eat and tell stories and laugh.

"I guess we are all People, when you get right down to it. We all need the same things."

"What things, exactly?" Mel asked with a sidelong glance.

"Well, I guess most of all, someone we trust to listen to us, that compassionate presence. And someone to share our passion—for art, for our work, for farming, for social justice, for whatever."

Our coffee cups were empty but we went on talking, too engrossed to go in for a second cup. We talked about many things. Darwin hauled the last load of manure and hosed down the equipment by himself.

Mel and I put together supper. While he cleaned himself up, I opened a Mason jar of canned cherries. He made us some sandwiches out of Trail Bologna and Swiss cheese. Just the kind of supper you'd expect to find in that house. Darwin ate in silence while the two of us made conversation without him.

"Thanksgiving's coming next week," I said.

Darwin looked up from his plate with interest at that. "Let's talk turkey," he said. By then it was perfectly clear he was angry that his "Angel" had been stolen by his own uncle right from under his nose.

"We should do Turkey Day here," Mel said, his eyes lighting up. It may have been out of our lingering sense of guilt or as a way to appease Darwin.

"Here? Could we do that?" I asked.

"Yeah, why not?" Mel said. "I'll just tell Mom I've got other plans. You can look around and see who doesn't have plans for the day, and I'll get a turkey. Just find some people who know how to cook though, because I'm not doing it all myself."

"I'll bring the zucchini," Darwin said. His humor was improving with this talk of Thanksgiving.

"Family happens!" I said lightheartedly. For me, making these plans was an affirmation that our lives would somehow come together in spite of the different paths we'd been traveling.

Mel quoted a Bible verse: "All things are possible." I didn't remember it all, but just the first few words were enough to take me forward. As he'd said before, Moment by moment is how we live our lives. And in each moment is hidden possibility.

Kairos—moments of grace and opportunity. They just kept coming.

ℯ

After you've been on a farm, its scent lingers on your clothes and shoes. Darwin showered before we left, but it was almost as if the odor had taken up residence in my body, and of course in my car. I can't say it was objectionable. The scent reminded me of a good and contented past.

When I got home, I headed for the tub, where I soaked in oil of lavender, my own healing herb, and began to push things around in my spirit. "Like Mel and Darwin cleaning out the barn," I thought wryly. But I knew in my heart something had shifted and I was no longer lost, confused, and angry.

I was also thinking about Mel's reflections on learning from the people he was trying to teach. They taught him more than he taught them, he'd surmised. "That's probably true for me too," I thought. "I learn a lot from my People."

The phone rang. My mother was calling from a pay phone in Honduras. I heard Latin music in the background and knew I couldn't tell her much except that I had made plans for celebrating Thanksgiving. She would miss the holiday, but she was in a warm climate and nothing could make her as thankful as she was for that. She told me about the dental clinics with the dentist volunteers, the air travel to La Mosquitia with a missionary pilot who'd weighed both her and the crate of eggs he'd bought at the gas station in Tegucigalpa. I listened and left news about my life unsaid for the time being. It would wait for her return.

That night in a dream my angel visited. She had no wings, but the light around her was dusted with something like rhinestones, pearls, or stars—maybe beads from a wedding gown. She was humming a nursery song about lavender. I felt as warm as I ever had. She gathered me up and cradled me in her lap. She was Goddess. So I clung to this motherly bosom of God. It was she who had led me to my homeplace, the place love inhabits. And I knew beyond all doubt that I was loved.

18

As the three of us sat talking in the kitchen, the Thanksgiving guest list kept expanding. Besides Rhonda and Dale, we'd invited Darwin, Kyra, and Joe and Erika, who were both too far from their families to get home for the holiday weekend. At the last minute we added Ellen and Lou Miller to the guest list, because Rhonda found out they didn't have anyplace to go and she suspected their food stamps would be gone long before the end of the month.

"You know, it's a bit of a sacrifice giving up the big feast my family puts on every year," Mel said, shaking his head ruefully. I knew he was just giving us a hard time. I'm sure Darwin did too.

"I've been to those dinners. Quite something," Darwin said, appreciatively rubbing his stomach.

"Don't you worry a bit," I told him. "I think we can put together a feast everyone will like. I admit it might not be quite what the Martins do, but at least we're sure we'll have plenty of zucchini bread."

My prediction turned out to be true. Rhonda and I ended up being on the phone every day, putting together a menu that would compete with anyone's spread. At least we thought so.

Mel was to cook the turkey and make bread stuffing from a traditional recipe he promised to get from his mother, but when he told her he wasn't coming to her dinner, and why, she'd insisted on coming over to the homeplace to clean and help make the stuffing Wednesday afternoon.

I volunteered to make cranberry relish. That required no more work than grinding the tart, red berries along with an orange—peel and all—and then adding plenty of sugar.

Besides the mashed potatoes, which would be a group effort on Thursday morning, Rhonda and I were bringing several other dishes that would be ready to stick in the oven. Darwin promised to bake a fresh batch of zucchini muffins and would also assemble a zucchini casserole from remnants of his crop.

Kyra insisted on bringing dinner rolls, although she kept apologizing that she'd have to purchase them at the bakery. My pumpkin pies were a triumph, despite my long hiatus as a cook. I would whip real cream for the topping, straight from the in-house dairy. No artificial white stuff this time.

On Wednesday afternoon, Rhonda and Dale came by and picked everyone up. It was the best plan we could come up with, and this time no one would get lost. Dale was glad to provide a van from the dealership where he worked. Rhonda kept things lively as we traveled the now familiar roads south to Mel's farm.

I felt good thinking about the prospect of spending a weekend with all these friends. If I was feeling good, I'm sure for others this was a highlight. Some of them didn't get out of Hilldale very often, so a trip like this was noteworthy for them. Besides looking forward to the meal, we would shrug off the artificial boundaries that confined us and come together just as people. I knew there were probably administrators at Helping Hands who wouldn't approve, but the rigid rules of the past were making way for a fresh start for all of us. If I had to explain it to someone, I would.

Each person coming had some connection to the others. Besides Kyra and Darwin, who were on my case-management roster, we invited Ellen and Lou, a married couple who were both service recipients from our system. They had another connection too. They'd been attending the Church of the Crucified Redeemer. Ellen especially seemed to enjoy the singing there. Both rarely missed a service, and I knew they appreciated the visitors' meal served by the church one Sunday each month. Rhonda, as she has with so many others who come to the church, seemed to have taken them into her heart. No one probably really knew all the help she gave them. I was glad we could include them in our Thanksgiving.

The van was full by the time we'd picked up everyone with their overnight luggage and food. Mel had assured us it would be fun to come early and stay overnight. He'd planned a wiener roast and would burn logs from an old apple tree.

In the van, Rhonda brought out her ukulele, and before we knew it she had us singing camp songs and other silly songs from childhood that you almost forget. It seemed that no matter what song someone started, there was always another one waiting to be sung.

My heart was light and free as we laughed and sang, making our way down the road. None of us thought about differences in social status. We were all People. We forgot our labels for the time being and enjoyed being just who we were: friends and companions on a journey, celebrating a holiday and our own individual lives, looking forward to turkey and dressing and pumpkin pie.

Out ahead, the red sun was sinking lower by the minute behind the rolling hills. The road stretched out like a ribbon, shimmering in the glow. When I closed my eyes, it was as if we were floating. We were being carried along by a tide of good will and community spirit. We were riding behind the eye of a video camera, the hills unrolling themselves before us. The dormant fields were brown and quiet in the setting sun, but the sky was bright and warm; pinks and blues and lavenders across the horizon tried to get our attention.

Somehow it felt right that my love for Mel also stretched wide to touch the lives of Darwin, Kyra, Joe and Erika, Ellen and Lou, and of course Rhonda and Dale—particularly Rhonda, who had been part of this journey for so many months. It seemed right that Mel was giving all of us the opportunity to share an old-fashioned Thanksgiving on his farm. In the back two seats of the van, our passengers quit singing and began talking about the sights they saw along the way and memories of other trips out of town.

Kyra was quiet. I had a fleeting concern that her ever-present paranoia was making it difficult for her to enjoy riding in the van, but I hoped that maybe she too was simply taking in the beauty of creation.

The van groaned up the steep driveway to Mel's house and eased to a stop under the old pine tree. We roused ourselves to gather our belongings and the assorted baskets and boxes containing tomorrow's food. The dark porch was accented by two bamboo patio torches stuck in the ground at an angle near the steps to the farmhouse. Inside, the house was also well lighted, for once. As we stepped in, the subtle aroma of sage and onion greeted us. There was also just a hint of garlic and fish sauce lingering in the kitchen, but there was no mistaking it was Thanksgiving!

"Umm! I smell stuffing," I exclaimed as Mel reached for my arm. He seemed eager to touch me, but in the presence of all our friends he only took my elbow and guided me to the table, reaching for my plastic carrier as he did so. Everyone dropped their food onto the table, and

Rhonda and I busied ourselves putting things away. The pies went into the refrigerator, but some of the other things were placed on a table on the screened porch off the kitchen. In the fall weather, it served as an overflow refrigerator.

"I've got everything set up outside for tonight," Mel said. "Would anyone like a blanket before we go out to the orchard?" It was one of the delights of that warm autumn: we were still able to spend an evening outdoors. He had a spread of hot dogs, fixings, marshmallows, and a gallon of cider lined up on a hay wagon that served as a table. As we huddled close around the fire or sat on the makeshift seating Mel had put out for us, we continued the talk while we ate.

"This is a nice spread you've got here," said Joe. He gestured across the fields toward the road with a sweep of his arm. "It feels neighborly to me."

That was a signal to Mel to tell one of his stories. Thankfully, a funny one this time. "The neighbors here are self-reliant," he began. "Yet everyone helps everyone else. That's one of the best things about living here. And everyone has a garden and puts up fruits and vegetables for winter. The neighbors drive up and down this road and they can tell you a story about everyone who lives along here. There are probably hundreds of stories they can tell. They tell them to one another as they drive through the hills and kick up dust on the gravel roads that connect them.

"Outsiders, like you? Well, we never know when you'll become part of a story too.

"See, there was this farm couple, let's call them Grover and Maude. They had a truck patch way bigger than mine over there. And one day a traveling salesman selling stainless-steel cookware stops in and asks if they'd have a cookware party. That's how people do around here, at least how they did back then.

"It's a nice thing those cookware salesmen do. They bring all the food, and the pots and pans, and all you do if you're the host is set the table and invite a bunch of friends and relatives in. The salesmen do all the cooking."

"Sounds like us, coming here," I said.

"Yeah," said Erika. "That would be us, inviting ourselves to dinner."

"After dinner the salesman has plenty to tell you and your guests about the cookware and how it takes less water to cook in these pans with their tight-fitting lids, so you get more vitamins for your carrot. Before you know it, the salesman is writing up orders and the dinner guests are pulling out their checkbooks."

"Sounds like a classic example of momentum to compliance," said Dale, who probably used the same techniques every day. The rest of us didn't have a clue what he was talking about. Darwin asked him what it meant.

"Well," Dale explained, "if I accept something from you, then you will listen to my pitch. Next thing you know, we've got us a string of exchanges set up that leads to a final exchange—"

"And the cookware salesman has you signed on for a lifetime of painless stainless payments," Mel finished.

"That's pretty much what happens," Dale added.

Mel took off again with his narrative. I watched his face as he gathered us all into the story.

"Now, this family provided all the vegetables from the truck patch. The wife called up a bunch of the neighbors, invited everyone she could think of. For some reason everyone had plans. A birthday party for Dad, a ball game they had tickets for, a long-overdue shopping trip. It ended up that only one family could make it. That was Cletus and Sadie, who lived up the road a piece.

"Well, turns out this salesman, he's from up around

Cleveland somewheres. He chops up the peppers and stuff the family grows and stirs together a mighty terrific chicken paprikash using his own authentic seasoning. The smell is wonderful. The hosts-turned-guests are used to eating plain stuff like pot roast, fried potatoes, or sausage gravy and biscuits.

"After they say grace, everyone starts eating. Then all of a sudden ol' Cletus—who's always been kind of ailing anyway—can't get his breath—starts coughing and sputtering. Everyone wonders if he's choking. But no, seems like he just has a terrible allergy to paprika. So he's in such a panic he starts to hyperventilate. Everyone's terrified, 'specially the peddler.

"They call the rescue squad from Haysville, and pretty soon they come barrelin' up the road, sirens wailin'. The paramedics give Cletus a paper bag to breathe in and a shot of some anti-allergy stuff, and he calms right down.

"Next thing you know, there's a lot more people in the house. The neighbors have magically returned just in time from their shopping, ball game, and birthday party. Just in time to stop by and see what happened.

"The salesman adds some water and turns up the heat. Maude finds more plates and silverware, and everyone has a taste of the paprikash. Those very neighbors are probably getting all those pans out *right now,* to cook Thanksgiving dinner. It's been decades since that happened but that stainless cookware lasts a lifetime. Probably won't be cookin' paprikash. Least ways not at Sadie and Cletus's house."

"Quite a story, Mel," said Rhonda. "Reminds me of Uncle Elmer."

"Yeah, Elmer! Gotta tell you about Elmer." Rhonda's bait was all it took to launch another one of Mel's stories. He was just hitting his stride, it seemed.

Everyone lounged close to the fire to stay warm, but

from time to time someone got up to skewer a couple more marshmallows on a long fork. Some were patient to a fault and produced golden-brown, melting confections in the embers that had died down to a red-hot glow. Others preferred the char-blazed version and let their mini torches glow a second or so before blowing out the flames and crunching the blackened shells.

"Uncle Elmer, well, Uncle Elmer is in Hilldale Christmas shopping a few years ago. Planned on buying his wife, Trudy, a new robe. There he is, a little out of his element, in Freeds, the biggest department store in town. He's headed toward the lingerie department when who should he bump into but Great-aunt Ada.

"'Ada,' he says to her, 'So good to see you. Hey, I'm on my way to buy Trudy a robe for Christmas. How 'bout helping me pick it out?'

"Now, I don't know if Elmer needs help or just wants to humor his wife's great-aunt. Anyway Ada seems flattered and leads the way, swinging her cane as they walk through the store and take the elevator to the second floor.

"So the pair, they have a great time in the store looking at all the holiday displays, stopping off to watch kids talk with Santa, and sampling free hot chocolate. They sit a while on the bench near the Christmas tree, resting and catching up on family gossip. 'Course it's Elmer who does most of the talking.

"Then they shop until they find the perfect robe. It costs way more than he usually spends, but it's Christmas and I guess Great-aunt Ada is a pretty good influence on him. Elmer agrees to have it gift-wrapped—it was free back in those days—and they part at the revolving door. Elmer has a foil-wrapped package with a big red bow on it.

"'By the way,' he tells Trudy later on that evening at

supper. 'Guess who I saw in Freeds when I was buying your gift?'

"'Who?'

"'I bumped into your aunt Ada in there. We had a wonderful visit. She even helped pick out your gift.'

"'Elmer,' his wife Trudy says, 'I don't know who you was talking to, 'cause Ada, she's down in Sun City. Didn't I tell you they called and said she broke her hip and would be laid up all winter in the rehab center down there?'"

The fire was a pile of red and orange embers, and we were all tired and relaxed. I didn't believe Mel's stories for a minute, but that didn't matter. What mattered was that we were all together, laughing and making memories. That's exactly what it means to be at home. And it could happen to a group like ours just as much as it could happen to any family group sitting around a fire—or sharing a plate of paprikash, for that matter.

It was late. Rhonda and I helped Mel round up several comforters and pillows, and we discussed where everyone would sleep. There were three bedrooms upstairs and the living room, besides the small room I'd come to think of as mine.

After a while, even Darwin headed "up the wooden hill," and Mel declared he was ready to "hit the hay." He smiled that sort of crooked grin that was now so familiar. I could see it in my mind no matter where I was. But it felt so good not to have to imagine it just then.

On another day, I would try and try to remember each twist and turn of Mel's stories. But I would never succeed in telling them the way he did. There was only one Mel.

And I suspected that his simple down-to-earth humor would stay with me always.

I would need the memory of that night more than I realized at the time. Those stories and the warmth I absorbed as we sat and listened would be with me in the cocoon, where we waited, as all of nature does, for spring-time, and the voice of love awakening from a winter that turned out to be longer than any I'd ever known.

Finally alone, Mel and I stepped out onto the porch to tend to the bamboo lanterns. He extinguished them and took my hand. At last he wrapped his arms around me, pressing his hands tightly into my back through my fleece jacket. We held each other close, our hearts beating as one.

"I love you, Angie. Do you know how much I love you?"

"Me too, I love you, too," I answered.

We stood there a long time, holding onto what we'd found.

The moon overhead was clear and bright, the air crisp and pungent with farm smells and the scent of earth and stars. From somewhere on the other side of the barn, a snowy owl called out, reminding me of the wisdom of being at home with my heart.

19

THE FARM AWAKENED EARLY, but the guests took their time. I got up with Mel before chore time, and the two of us prepared to wrestle the huge bird into an ancient enamelware roaster reclaimed from the large shelf above the cellar stairs. The roaster had been coated with black coal dust, and I'd scrubbed it with hot, soapy water.

Mel stuffed the turkey, which he said Paulie's Sarah had ordered fresh from an organic poultry farm an hour away, over in Columbiana, almost in Pennsylvania. Mel took a large darning needle and cotton string and trussed the cavity closed. He was in a hurry to get to the barn. Darwin, Dale, and Joe followed, without bothering to eat breakfast. The women were still sleeping, except for Erika, who appeared and looked ready to chore too.

"Come on out with us," Darwin told her. I saw a flirtatious spark waiting to ignite, but was sure Erika could handle it.

"There is so much to be thankful for," I thought. It was easier in the open spaces of the country to remember to be thankful. I was thankful for all the usual things: food, clothing, shelter, health, friends, family, and a community that looked after those who belonged there. I was thankful, probably more than most, for a healthy mind, because I'd seen what can happen when the mind isn't well.

Although I'd struggled with anxiety and even temporary depression, I'd been given so many opportunities to contribute. Maybe I *was* making the world a better place. My depression had been temporary, and I was pulling out of it. For others, it's a condition that has to be attended to every day of their lives. I thought of Kyra and the large pill sorter she carried with her in her signature velour bag. Her mind was kept together with the help of medical miracles. But it would heal a day at a time, as she continued on her path.

After the first preparations were completed, I wandered across the yard to the garlic garden. There was little to remind me of the bulbs resting in the rich soil. But I believed in the potential each bulb held. It was the old, old lesson, the way the cloves split off and carry within themselves the promise of more. The sagging frost-wilted stalks lay soggy and brown on the topsoil. Winter is for resting, but even in the coming dull, dark season, life force was surging within their husks. The roots were reaching down and the tops waited for time to come when they would stretch up.

I had somehow come to a new vision of human potential too. I smiled thinking about the journey to the farm. The silly songs, the laughter, the stories, and the contentment and goodwill that flowed around us as we traveled and shared the warmth. We were on a *kairos* journey, each of us traveling in God's time as we cultivated hope, sought our recovery, and moved forward.

I stood on the edge of the garden a long time, soaking up the early morning, chilly as it was. I knew it would come alive again—this brown memory of the giant cloves, strong beneath the surface. I planned then to paint from my memory the dormancy, rich and oily with the generous dream of all that is possible—even from the dirt. From hidden things, life springs.

By the time I'd wandered back to the house, the guests who weren't in the barn had finished eating their bowls of cold cereal and drinking their coffee or tea. Kyra carefully washed the dishes scattered around and then wandered into the living room, where she sat in the corner of a sofa and dozed, despite the early hour.

Mel reappeared clean-shaven and smelling of soap and drugstore aftershave. He and Rhonda began talking about going to the Thanksgiving church service.

"You're going to church this morning?" I asked incredulously. "But, what about our dinner?"

"Church starts at eleven. We get everything in the oven, set the table, and take off," said Mel.

"It's a tradition," said Rhonda.

I wouldn't argue with tradition, and I could see that Mel wanted us to go to his church, Plainview Mennonite.

Ellen and Lou offered to help by setting the table while Rhonda and I stood companionably beside one another at the sink, peeling potatoes. We were well aware that, other than the turkey, mashed potatoes and gravy were what everyone looked forward to, so we peeled an ample supply. I was thankful for Rhonda because I knew she had inherited a heaping helping of the genetic material that would supersede my own puny cooking skills.

Our dinner preparations went fabulously. By midmorning everything that could be fixed, arranged, or dished up was ready. The turkey was starting to brown and the potatoes were waiting on the back burner of the gas range. Mel asked again if anyone was going to church, and a few said yes.

"I'd been wondering how people manage to put a huge feast on the table and still attend church," I told Mel. "But from our own performance, I see it's possible. Sure, I'll go."

Rhonda and I left the dinner in the hands of the others. For my part, I had to admit that my motives were not altogether related to my desire to give thanks. I wanted to attend partly out of curiosity. I'd never been to a Mennonite church service, and I was secretly hoping to meet some of Mel's family or one or two of his friends.

§

The church was full, and we found a place to sit halfway up. The meeting place was beautiful in its simplicity. A large wooden cross hung on the wall behind a massive pulpit that sat on a platform rising several feet above the main floor. A communion table in front of the pulpit held a wicker cornucopia spilling over with small gourds, pumpkins, and Indian corn. The bright colors stood out against the white walls and light-colored wood pews. Two planters held artificial greenery. A spinet piano was turned sideways on the left at the front, but no one was playing it. The congregation sat silently waiting for the service to begin.

Soon the minister stood and opened the service with a short, spontaneous prayer that alluded to the rural community and the bounty we would partake of later in the day. A song leader stepped forward and announced the first hymn, "Come, Ye Thankful People."

I was amazed by the sound that came from that group of perhaps eighty people. They sang as if they were a choir, only more raw and less balanced, but in four-part harmony, unaccompanied. I listened to my soprano voice as it blended with Rhonda's strong alto harmony on one side of me and Mel's resonant tenor on the other. I hadn't expected him to be a singer. But then, in that room, it suddenly made perfect sense. In fact, many things made sense to me as I sat watching and listening to the Mennonites as they joined voices. My spirit too was caught up in the extemporaneous prayers that came from the life and heart of the worship leader—the voice of the people—instead of words from the liturgy of another time and place.

I listened, but at the same time my mind wandered during testimonies of thankfulness for safety during the harvest. There was also gratitude from a woman who had recently come through surgery for cancer. She was definite in her determination to "give all the glory to God." I joined my heart with the gathered community in prayers for a work team that would soon be going to Bolivia to help build a church.

I looked around at the people gathered there and finally let my eyes rest on the bright sunlight shining on an evergreen just outside the window of the sanctuary. A flock of geese drifted across the sky as we sang the final verse of the last hymn.

> For the joy of human love,
> Brother, sister, parent, child,
> Friends on earth and friends above,
> For all gentle thoughts and mild;
> Lord of all, to thee we raise
> This our hymn of grateful praise.

The service ended and members lingered on the steps of the church and in the parking lot. There was a lot of talking and laughing, but many of the women looked to be in a bit more of a hurry than their men. I noticed some urging their husbands to the car with a tug or an anxious look. Young children chased one another around the back of the building, and one or two made a quick pass through the cemetery before being called back by their parents.

We didn't stay long, just a few minutes, but it was enough time for Mel to introduce me to Paulie and Sarah and their youngest two boys, and to his parents, Jim and

Dorothy Martin. They were all of a kind, I thought. Friendly, yet a bit distant. It could have been shyness as much as anything, much like Mel on that first day we'd met in the dark farmhouse. Simple and serious, but capable of great love.

20

IN THE FADING TWILIGHT, the guests drifted across the farm in different directions. Ellen and Lou retired to their suite on the second floor for the privacy of their borrowed room. Kyra pulled a box of pastels and a sketchbook from her bag and stationed herself beside the window facing west to capture the clouds as the wash of color spilled over them in preparation for sunset.

I watched her effortless passage into the world she loved most. She had something I was only beginning to rediscover: the ability to move from living to her art, fluidly fading from reality to this other world in the movement of a hand. For her it happened naturally, a ritual that consisted of nothing more than lifting a box from its place and opening the cover of a sketchbook.

There was no pretentiousness or ego in her desire for expression. It was as simple as breathing. I admired that about her and knew enough to respect her solitude, though I longed to look over her shoulder and see what she was producing. I knew instinctively that she needed the privacy and security of open space around her. This solitude allowed her creativity to flourish, and I would no more intrude on that than I would barge in through Lou and Ellen's closed door.

I sat quietly in the opposite corner of the room, encased comfortably in an old wing chair that I'd claimed for my own on my first visit to the farm. The chair was worn, but it fit my own body perfectly and enfolded me, reminding me again of the comfort of this place that called out to me, as if I had never before experienced a chair or a shared meal, or enjoyed the laughter that comes on the heels of a well-told story.

I glanced toward Mel's bookshelf with its array of interesting titles. One or two tempted me, but instead I simply sank into the chair and enjoyed the view out the window, giving myself completely to the idleness of a holiday late-afternoon. I smiled to think that somewhere—everywhere—all over the country people were sitting in living rooms and family rooms watching football. Everywhere except here. And here, for us, it didn't matter. Our world was full of other things, more tangible and life-giving, but also more rare than most imagine.

Darwin and Mel had wandered out to the barn and outbuildings. It must have been hard for them to stay indoors when the air remained so warm and inviting. We all knew severe weather was on its way. And probably very soon. They had gone out on some pretense of looking at a project Mel had brewing in the shed, but I suspected that, as much as anything, they just wanted to enjoy the beautiful autumn afternoon and the crisp air that filled the lungs when one first stepped outside. And Darwin would probably have another smoke.

The dinner had been a huge success. Even more than the food, it had been the fellowship that we would all remember and cherish. Around the table there in Mel's comfortable farm kitchen we had melted into that something different I'd already begun to observe. Each of us had come home in some sense, as we shared the common things of life: good food, stories, and laughter, no matter how troubled we were.

Again, at dinner, I had been as much an observer as a participant. From my vantage point, sitting to the right of

Mel at the dining table, which had been stretched to its limit with the addition of two boards, I watched each of my friends and thought about their lives. I felt warmth spread through my spirit as I recalled how each of them in their brokenness had somehow become part of my own journey toward wholeness.

Maybe it was then I realized that my road had never really been a solitary one, but rather, becoming lost had been part of the journey I needed to take. It was, I decided, this unmapped exploration that had brought me to a new place, where I felt more at home than anywhere I'd been in my life.

It was not so much a physical place that I was thinking of. It was another place, where I could forget all the artificial limitations and conventions we set up to negotiate us carefully and securely through the world. Here though, at home, I'd found something different. This was a place of the heart I'd entered that called me to dive into the passion and mystery of life and to be fearless about doing so, despite the questions that still plagued me.

Rhonda wandered in and sat companionably in a rocking chair next to me. The antique creaked as she lowered herself into it. She propped a pillow behind her back to make herself comfortable in a chair that was much less hospitable than mine. She had a book in her hand and looked nearly as meditative as I was feeling.

"Happy?" she asked as she searched my face for some clue about where our conversation ought to go, or even if I wanted to talk.

"Oh, yes!" I exclaimed. "So truly happy! Finally!"

Rhonda nodded and waited for me to continue.

"I never knew I could feel so good, so peaceful, so whole. What has happened to me? I only know and feel that something is so different now."

"You're in love, Angie. That's what happened." She smiled and I was suddenly conscious of her eyes—deep, brown pools that held me in their warmth. I felt close to Rhonda, my spiritual guide, my woman of wisdom. She was so much more to me than just a friend. It was as if she were a mother to me in some way—a spiritual mother, maybe. She had guided me through the maze of questions in my painful recovery from a past that was littered with unhappiness and buried sorrow. She had done it gently as she listened and cared and challenged me to take the next step.

"It's not just Mel that I love, Rhonda," I said simply.

"I know, Angie. I know."

I looked at her and smiled, and our eyes brimmed over with tears. She glanced down at the cover of the book in her hand. It had the word *Desert* in the title. I had traveled through a desert. She had been my guide.

"You've been transformed, Angie. You've awakened and tasted grace. It is not something everyone is willing to experience, this journey you've taken. It's an adventure, really. At times I watched and it seemed you were almost being dragged to the place where you are now, dragged kicking and screaming. But you took the journey. You jumped into the river and found you could swim. Now you are able to see the holy in all of life—in your experiences and in the lives of others, especially in the lives of the brokenhearted ones. They are the ones, after all, who truly know the way to God. And that may lead us through suffering, as you now know.

"'Blessed are the brokenhearted, for they shall see God.'

"And somehow," she continued, "when hope and healing are offered through our compassionate presence— in the form of a listening ear, a word of encouragement, a hug, even a good meal, a story, or a glass of water—the mystery of God can burst in on us and move us to become something new and radically different. Someone like you, Angie, filled with grace and love.

I smiled at her, still tearful.

"Now, pass along the love you have experienced from God and others. That is how you will find your life suddenly alive with meaning as it never has before."

I nodded in response to her benediction and sat in silence, taking in all she said. I knew the truth of her words, although I couldn't have said it as she did. It is, after all, the gift of a spiritual leader to put words to faith. But also her gift to love me and to guide me on the journey. I knew that she, more than anyone, had brought me to this place of wholeness. I'd always be grateful to her.

"Want to take a walk?" she asked, shifting in her creaking rocker.

"Sure, let me grab my jacket."

℮

"Mel and Darwin are probably out there in the shed, tinkering with that bomb tractor," Rhonda said, laughing.

"Bomb tractor? What do you mean? I've heard of calling a hot rod a bomb, but I've never heard of a bomb tractor."

"You'll see soon enough," she said.

We took the path near the garden and headed toward the back pasture. I hoped to find Sugar and Lightning enjoying this last day of warmth before winter would take over and send them into the barn for the next few months. Buster came bursting from behind the house, galloping and barking at us as he came.

"Didn't Mel tell you about his tractor?" Rhonda asked me.

"Well, no. I guess not. I mean, I know about his John Deere, but I never heard him call it a bomb tractor. Does he have some other tractor somewhere?"

"I figured you knew all about it."

I lunged sideways to avoid a huge thistle, elegant with purple blossoms, that was crowding me off the path.

"Mel's been trying to invent something that will diffuse the bombies so that the farmers in Laos can till their rice paddies again. He's been working off and on for several years on the project. Haven't you noticed how he has all those manuals and notebooks and reports all over his desk?" Rhonda asked me.

"Well, I did notice, but I never put that together with a project like this. He did tell me about the bombies and his great concern about all of that. I know the feelings he has for the Lao people are deep. And for the land. Neither love is ever far from his mind. It seems as if those few years he lived there shaped his whole view of the world, and of life."

"I know. Ever since I first met Mel back in high school, I knew he was someone special. He wasn't the greatest student or anything back then. In fact he was one of those guys we used to call 'the flannels' because they wore flannel shirts and jeans to school all the time. That was back when most guys wore dress pants to school. But Mel and his crowd wore jeans, and they were always hanging out in the shop, welding something or fixing up an old go-cart. Mel never quite fit in with that crowd though, not completely. His interest in literature seemed at odds somehow with the way he was otherwise. I suppose something like that seems more unique when you're in high school than when you're older."

"The first time I was here," I said, "I started to walk toward that shed, the one out behind the barn with the trumpet vine growing up over the tin roof, and I noticed there was a padlock on the door. About that time Mel got real strange and headed me off in another direction. It was like he didn't want to talk about it or show me. Like it was some big secret or something. And one other time too when we got near it, he just talked about appropriate technology and was pretty vague about what he was doing in there. I was starting to think there was an arsenal or that he had some strange collection or something."

"Oh, no, it's nothing like that," Rhonda said, laughing. "He's just sort of humble about what he's doing. Plus, I think he isn't sure he's really on the right track with this whole thing. I've been reading about land mines—this desecration thing—in *A Common Place*, the peace-and-justice magazine I subscribe to. It's such a tragedy, yet hardly anyone wants to even admit it happened, let alone find a way to deal with the tremendous damage these cluster bombs have done to the farmlands in Laos. It's probably going to be a much bigger project than Mel thinks. The article I read said a British group called the Mines Advisory Council has some kind of device that will locate and then uncover and detonate the bombies. That's essentially what Mel is trying to do with the tractor. But along with the device on the front of the tractor, he has to figure out a way to protect the driver, while still allowing the driver to see where he's going. It sounds complicated to me, but knowing Mel and his mechanical genius, I'm sure he'll come up with something."

Rhonda's insight into Mel's creative efforts surprised me. I knew he enjoyed tinkering, but I hadn't realized it was this serious. "How do you know so much about all of this? I'd never even heard about the damage to the farmlands over there until Mel told me about it."

"Well, I guess for me it's from reading some of the

religious papers that come through the office. Mel is a Mennonite, as you know, and they're really into some of these issues of justice. They're conscientious objectors, but for many of them it goes way beyond protesting war or avoiding military service. They make it a whole way of life. And that can include something as practical as building a tractor or taking a vacation to a third-world country to help construct a church building."

"I was thinking about that this morning in their Thanksgiving service," I said. "The things people talked about there. There's something neat about that. I wish I could find some people who were as concerned about the injustice here at home and about the kind of bombies that make normal life so difficult for people like Kyra and Darwin."

"I know," Rhonda said, kicking a stone ahead of her in the path. "I think some of them care about those issues too. It's just easier a lot of the time to do something tangible —give a basket of food, or something. For some reason, it seems more important if the need is far away. Still, people like Mel are hard to find. I hope you realize what a gem he is."

"Oh, I do," I said. I felt a sudden urge to touch her, to let her know what a wonderful friend she was to me and how much I cared for her. I put my hand on her shoulder as we draped ourselves over the fence and watched the horses. They were way across the pasture and didn't even see us at first.

"Just don't get too close to that arsenal of his," Rhonda said, laughing.

"I thought you told me he doesn't have an arsenal."

"Well, he does, sort of. He showed me a whole crate of those bombies in the back corner of the shed. I was horrified that he had them there like that. And they're real too. I don't know how he ever managed to get them. But I guess he needs them to test the contraption he's building to see if it really works. Maybe that's why he didn't show you. He's probably a little concerned about who knows he has them. Of course he can trust you. Maybe he's just careful out of habit."

"I suppose that could be true," I said slowly. "But I'm a little hurt that you seem to know so much about this and I hardly know anything."

"Well, now maybe you know how Darwin felt when you two kept him in the dark about your blossoming romance," Rhonda said, looking sidewise at me. "About that tractor, you're going to learn a lot more pretty fast," she said, pointing in the direction of the barn.

A medium-sized, red tractor was heading toward us. I strained to see who was driving but couldn't tell. A sturdy, steel frame had been attached to the tractor and completely encased the driver. A sort of auger-shaped contraption was mounted onto the front, but it wasn't touching the ground. As the tractor roared closer, I saw Mel inside his armored vehicle. He was laughing and let the door swing open as he came closer.

"How do you like my garlic harvester?" he asked me.

"You are a real mystery man," I said. "Here all this time I thought you were hiding a collection of classic cars, and really you're inventing a radical piece of farm equipment."

"It's radical, all right," quipped Mel. "Want a ride?"

"No, I'll pass this time. Thanks anyway."

For months afterward, I'd be playing that scene over in my mind. I would remember the light banter between us, the crooked smile that lit up his face, the lines around his eyes set there by years of squinting into the sun. I'd remember the sound of his voice as it had been that afternoon. Somehow I was able to take it all in—just this ordinary exchange. Maybe it was because I hadn't known about the tractor before, and it was all new to me. I was so grateful later on for that memory and that encounter.

"See you back at the barn," I said. "By the way, where's Darwin?" I was still such a caretaker, even now worrying about Darwin.

"Oh, he's back there. We were just trying to fit the lift onto this thing so we can try it out one of these days. I think I'll go on back. Why don't you make yourselves useful and get those horses to come over here. It's supposed to get cold tonight—maybe even snow toward morning—and Sugar and Lightning are going to have to kiss this pasture good-bye."

"Sure, we'll get them. But it might take us a while," said Rhonda.

Mel whistled. The steeds pricked up their ears and trotted our way. My heart quickened at the thought of leading the horses back to the barn. Again, that good feeling, the one that has been with me ever since I'd arrived the evening before. It was a feeling of contentment at knowing I was finally home. It was somehow tied up with putting my hand on the halter of a horse and leading him through a gate. Home was here in the laughter and friendly banter between friends. It was in the very act of leaning on a fence, kicking a stone down a path, dodging a cow pie, or letting my eyes follow the flight of the Canada geese who didn't bother flying south. Home is a man on a tractor, driving back to the barn at the end of a season. The very essence of Thanksgiving.

I caught Lightning, watched the tractor, and gave thanks all at once.

21

LIFE CAN CHANGE, and in a split second, everything you know and believe in is gone. In place of all that's familiar and loved is a gaping hole. That's how it was that Thanksgiving evening. One minute Rhonda and I were walking calmly down the lane, leading the horses back to their stalls. The next, our hearts were pounding with terror.

From the direction of the shed a loud explosion rocked the earth. It reverberated through the surrounding hills and shook the fence posts. Black smoke poured into the serene November sky, and pieces of stone and earth, grass and weeds, flew everywhere. A large clod of earth landed in front of us on the path.

Rhonda and I froze, and the horses reared and broke loose from our grip. We stood completely still as that explosion rocked our world. In the silence that came next, I knew a kind of terror I'd never known. My heart was pounding, while there was another great stillness—both inside me and in the world around.

Since that moment, I have thought that shock is a kind of blessing that gets you through trauma. Without it we would die. Shock set in almost immediately. I remember dropping to my knees as I heard the loud bang of the tin roof of the shed crashing down in front of me. The sound of the tractor died out in the same moment. As earth, rocks, and pieces of metal settled onto the ground, my knees gave way and I fell, face down in the rough, brown grass beside the path.

I smelled its faded beauty and felt the rough fronds against my cheek as I lay there strangely unknowing, and yet knowing all. I knew that soon I would rise and run. Soon I would go investigate. Soon the truth would be lying silent beside me. I felt a trickle of something running down my arm. Was it blood or sweat? I didn't know, and at that moment, I didn't care.

"Oh, God. Oh, God. My Jesus, mercy!" I heard myself cry out. But I will never know if the words were audible. I lay there with my hands outstretched, and my face in the grass of that fencerow for what seemed like forever, but might have been only a minute.

Off in the distance, I heard a dog bark. I heard Darwin yelling in the kind of voice I'd never heard anyone use. A desperate, fearful howl in the darkness, over and over the two repeated words: "Help me! Help me!" And I knew that whatever help he needed, I would not be able to give. I reached into the strength that had been growing inside me, an unknown and unseen force. I summoned it and lifted my head.

Despite my initial shock, the memory of every sight and sound is as clear in my mind as if it happened yesterday. Rhonda was running toward the shed, yelling to Darwin, whose figure was black. Blood was streaming from his face and arms, and his clothing was torn. He ran with a halting, strange gait that I've never seen anyone use. Rhonda yelled over her shoulder, "Call 9-1-1! Call 9-1-1! Get the cell phone! It's in the van!"

I was on my feet, running toward the van and taking in the devastation that stretched out in a wide circle from the shed. Dale, Rhonda's husband, appeared from the house and hollered, "I already called!"

A gaping hole remained where the back end of the shed had once been. Debris was strewn through the corn stubble, and some of it was on fire. The red tractor had tipped over on its side, the front wheels still turning. In a split second, I took in the still form of Mel, who had been ejected through the unlatched door of his bomb-proofed machine. He lay buried under wood and metal shards from the shed, just clear of the tractor that had come to rest on its side, a few feet away. Its front wheels were still turning.

Dale ran toward the tractor, thinking only about Mel, not the potential for an exploding fuel tank. Miraculously, it didn't explode. He went to Mel and started taking his pulse. He was bleeding from a large gash on his cheek and moaning. I wondered if Dale would try to move him, but he didn't. He counted heartbeats, then pulled off his shirt and pressed it to the gash on Mel's face to stop the bleeding.

Rhonda and I stood by helplessly with Darwin beside us. He was bleeding too, and said his ankle hurt but was remarkably aware of what was happening.

Time stood still. I do not remember much of the next minutes or hours. There was a crater from the explosion of the stack of bombies that had been lying in a heap for months. The bombies are full of sharp shards of metal, and these were scattered everywhere. Near the site of the accident, the metal clogged the path and spoke of destruction.

The ambulance from Haysville came roaring up the driveway, sirens blaring. Following the ambulance was a tanker truck. The rescue squad took over, and we stepped back to watch as they tended to Mel and Darwin. Others worked to contain the fire and soon had it extinguished. After what seemed much too long to the onlookers, they carefully lifted Mel and strapped him to a body board before placing him on a gurney. I could see that one leg was severely fractured and lacerated. I tried to stay out of the way.

Finally the emergency vehicles went screaming off with

Mel and Darwin, who would need X-rays and stitches. Rhonda and Dale led the rest of us back into the house. Dale told everyone to gather their things, and we decided he would take the rest back to Hilldale and their homes, while Rhonda and I would take Mel's truck to the Hilldale Medical Center.

ℰ

Later that day we would piece together how the explosion had happened. I suppose we can never be completely sure what caused it, but it seemed likely that Darwin had foolishly forgotten to extinguish a cigarette, which had ignited some brush behind the shed, which in turn had ignited the explosives. Fortunately, unlike the victims of land mines, all of us were somehow prevented from being harmed by the flying shrapnel. In fact, the most seriously injured was Mel. His bomb tractor might have protected him, although the force of the explosion caused it to roll. He'd been thrown clear through its open side door—open, I realized days later, because of me.

While Darwin's injuries looked superficial—a few cuts and scrapes, no broken bones—the greater injury would be from the knowledge he'd caused the devastation. But in the aftermath of the accident, his cognitive process had closed down. Of that I'm certain.

One always thinks later of ways everything could have been different. We could have asked Darwin to walk out to the pasture with us. We could have stopped by the shed and watched them work. Maybe we'd have noticed that Darwin was outside smoking and we would have stopped him. Why hadn't Mel warned him about smoking around the shed? Or had he, and that's why Darwin stepped outside? I should have cautioned Darwin about smoking on the farm. Why didn't I work with him more to stop smoking, knowing the many dangers it could pose out there? There were a thousand thoughts like this later. And not just mine. Each of us had our own set of whys.

Most of that long night, I sat in the waiting room. James and Dorothy were the first to arrive, then Paulie and Sarah along with two of their sons. Rhonda huddled with us. Gradually others drifted in. The small waiting room filled with relatives and church members. All of them, men and women alike, were dressed simply in denim and comfortable knits. The women wore skirts and comfortable shoes. The older women looked weary from the absence of makeup and too many hours in their holiday kitchens.

I looked around for Darwin, whose familiar face would have been welcome, but he wasn't there. I knew he was in the hospital, but he was still being attended to in the emergency room. I considered going to look for him, but couldn't make myself. Rhonda sat across from me. Her pants were grass stained and there was a hole in the knee where she'd fallen. My athletic shoes were spotted with blood stains but I had no idea how they'd gotten there.

My mind was alternately dull and blank, then alive and struggling to take in all that had happened. I caught the eye of Mel's father as he shifted in the waiting room chair that was too small to comfortably accommodate his large frame. He looked pale and tense. Just then a nurse came to the desk and picked up a clip board.

"Mr. Martin? Would you step this way, please?" He rose and walked toward her. Dorothy and Paulie followed. "Dr. Marthey says two of you may step into ICU for a five minute visit."

"Who wants to come with me?" James Martin asked.

I saw Dorothy shrink backward and Paulie step forward. I suspected that Dorothy was reluctant to see her son hooked up to machines and monitors, although she obviously loved him dearly. She hesitated briefly, then dropped back and leaned against a wall and fanned her flushed face with a medical brochure, as the two walked resolutely toward the large double doors.

Doug Rohrer, the pastor at Plainview Mennonite, took her arm and guided her back toward the chair she'd been sitting in. "Folks. Let's gather together and have a word of prayer on behalf of our brother, Mel." Doug had arrived just moments before and I could see the relief on faces around me when he stepped in wearing his chaplain's badge. His voice was mellow and resonant. Those who were sitting stood and someone reached for my hand. Then we joined hand to hand around the circle. Our heads bowed in unison.

"Lord, we come before you in humility, asking that you have mercy and look now on your servant Mel. We pray for his healing and that your will be done. Extend your hand of guidance as the doctors minister to the needs of our brother. Give them wisdom and strength. Help us to have faith and to trust you that all things work together for good to them that love God and are called according to his purpose. Guide and direct us as we walk into this unknown future we share as your people. God, we know that with you all things are possible and we pray if it be your will, you might grant brother Mel a speedy recovery so that he may once again work for your kingdom and bring others to a saving knowledge of Jesus Christ. We will give you all the glory. In the name of our Lord and Savior Jesus Christ we pray. Amen."

Rhonda squeezed me, and we both began to cry as we thought about the fragile breaths and the proximity of death on the other side of the large hospital doors. Doug Rohrer's words, though unfamiliar in their phrasing, had comforted me and released our tension. Perhaps it was the sound of his voice, the rhythm of the prayer and the warmth of the setting as we held one another's hands, I don't know. Maybe his prayer was being answered even then.

During the next couple of hours, as I sat there surrounded by Mel's people, I reviewed each moment I could remember from our brief friendship. I traveled back in time and revisited the forming of the special relationship between us. It was so new that no one here, except Rhonda and perhaps Paulie and Sarah, suspected the bond we shared. I felt awkward and alone. Rhonda's arm rested on the arm rest or our closely spaced chairs spilled over onto mine, as if to reassure me.

I played over the intimate moments Mel and I had spent together. They seemed like scenes from a movie. I imagined each detail, remembered the words that were said, the food that was eaten, the laughter and stories that were told. Most of all I remembered Mel's smile as he sat beside me or across from me. How he entertained me and drew me into his circle of compassion that was a thousand times more real than my own attempted caring gestures as I'd tried to help my People. I thought how his presence rippled out from his center in ways I'd never imagined until I saw the crowd gathered with me in this room. And how the love we shared was wide and inclusive and belonged not just to us, but to all who were part of our circles of life.

I prayed, too, just a little inward prayer repeated over and over. I had little confidence in my prayers. They were a sincere, if immature plea: "God, please help! Please help!"

James and Paulie emerged from the ICU. Everyone turned toward them and studied their faces for some clue, but there seemed to be little I could interpret. The men walked toward their wives and sat down in chairs beside them. The room got quiet as the rest of us tried to overhear their hushed conversation. Rhonda got up and walked to the water cooler at the far end of the room. She stopped to talk to the men briefly, then came back to me and held out a paper cup.

"Let's see if we can find out anything about Darwin," she said. I nodded and got up to follow her out into the hall.

As I'd suspected, he was still in the emergency room and was about to be released. "We still don't know much about how Mel's doing," I told him. Darwin nodded and dropped his eyes to the floor. "Everything's going to be okay," I said to him, wishing so much I could be certain it was true.

"Let's go to the cafeteria," suggested Rhonda. "I could use some coffee."

We followed her down the hallway and past the waiting room door. James and Dorothy emerged and greeted us.

"How is he?" Rhonda queried. "What did you find out?"

I felt my stomach flip flop as I imagined what I would hear in the reply.

"We don't know for sure," James said. "Lots of tubes and monitors. They're giving him blood and oxygen. Morphine and sedatives in his IV. His leg is really bad, but they suspect internal injuries. Still waiting for some X-rays. His one eye is swollen and I think they said they put in—what was it?—twenty-eight stitches in his face?"

"You said thirty-eight last time," reminded Dorothy.

"I don't know, but he looks horrible. I think his jaw was broken or something, along with the deep cuts on the left side of his face. We're just lucky that tractor didn't burst into flames with all the sparks from the shed burning."

I glanced at Rhonda and suddenly noticed the sooty layer of grime on her once-white blouse.

"What is the doctor saying?" I asked.

"They're more worried about his leg," James said.

Dale strode up the hall just then. He'd returned from taking the others back to Hilldale. Rhonda looked relieved to see him.

"How is he?" Dale asked.

"Not good at all," James continued. "They said he has multiple fractures. I can't remember which leg it is, but it was the femur in two places and the ankle too. I think they said it was crushed. Really, they said they hoped they could operate but it's too soon to tell how it's going to be."

"The doctor said he could lose his leg," Dorothy said. Her voice came in a rush with a breathless, overburdened energy.

"Now, Dorothy, we don't know that for sure. That was just something they mentioned. They have to prepare for the worst, you know. But Dr. Marthey was hopeful they can save it. It depends a lot on where the fractures are in relation to one another and how badly the ankle is mangled. We just don't know enough yet, and won't until they can get him stabilized. They're going to life-flight him to Cleveland."

My heart sank as I listened. I longed to be on the inner circle where Mel was concerned. I wanted to see him. Just see him, no matter how bad it was, or how horrid he looked, right then I just wanted to see him—to reassure myself he'd be okay. To squeeze his familiar farm-worn hand and let him know I'd be there for him. No matter what.

Rhonda must have understood my need. She also knew I needed to confirm my status in the hierarchy of family visitors. "You know, Angie here is a special person. She's a social worker and everything. I know she'd be happy to help out if you need someone to drive to Cleveland with you or anything."

I could have hugged Rhonda for the way she'd finessed it.

"Mel and I just got to be good friends lately," I said. "I was working with his nephew Darwin and we kind of hit it off."

"Oh, are you the girlfriend, then?" There was a faint suggestion of a twinkle in James' eyes.

"You might say that," I affirmed modestly. "And, I would be happy to help out if there's anything I could do."

"Well, thank you," said Dorothy. Her words were sincere, but their bluntness bothered me. Maybe the reserve in her voice was something akin to humility.

By now we'd forgotten the quest for coffee and when Mel's parents walked into the waiting room, Rhonda, Dale and I followed. Darwin hung back. I should have been looking out for him. Instead, he wandered off down the hospital corridor. Hours later, when I realized he wasn't with us, I finally found him after midnight, sleeping on a pew in the hospital chapel.

Back in the ICU waiting room, I found a chair and settled down to wait for more news. Pastor Rohrer paced back and forth between the groups of people. He wore no clerical garb and didn't hold a Bible in his hand, yet he was obviously speaking simple words of comfort and hope to those gathered around. Before he left for home he once again gathered all of us together for prayer. We stood in a circle, held hands, and prayed. By now everyone knew the extent of Mel's injuries. There were loud sniffles, and the simple words seemed to prompt men and women alike to let go of the tears that had been gathering like storm clouds behind their eyelids. I saw several men pull handkerchiefs from their pockets and wipe their faces, unobtrusively.

One of the older men started singing a hymn softly and before long everyone joined in. Even me. "Abide with me . . ." It was one of the hymns from my childhood, but I remembered the words mostly from the movie *Titanic*, making it seem even more poignant than it might have been for these others who, if they remembered the song from the movie, likely wouldn't have associated it with that disaster.

But for me, the words settled into a deep place and lodged themselves. "Help of the helpless, oh, abide with me."

The hymn spoke of courage, trust and faith that looked to a God who could do all things. The people in that room sang song after song, until I thought perhaps Mel could hear us. Maybe his spirit was spinning out from the unconscious state he presently was resting in, and he heard this plea for mercy by a community that obviously loved and had nurtured him for so many years.

I was in that room, sitting on a worn, upholstered chair that had held many who waited anxiously for news. Finally a doctor came through the double doors and stood in front of us, white coat buttoned up and stethoscope hanging like a medallion around her neck.

"I'm sorry . . ."

I didn't want to hear the next words. I wanted to stop my ears from hearing the doctor's summary of the past few hours. Stop time from moving on. Stop my own heart from beating. Stop the world from moving, the earth from spinning. But the words came.

There will be losses we will all need to endure. And waiting that will not be over for perhaps months. But we will go on, and this community of people will make that possible.

There was a path of some kind twisting and turning as it took us down the road that stretched ahead of us. That we knew. Rhonda reminded me of this when we finally left the Hilldale Medical Center the next day. Mel was being flown to Cleveland University Hospital, where the doctor hoped to keep him stabilized and in a drug-induced coma that would keep him immobile. They would try to find out the extent of his head injuries and assess the best course of action for dealing with the multiple fractures. There was a chance, the doctor wanted us to know, that Mel might lose the lower part of his left leg, but they would do everything in their power to try to save it.

I heard everything she said, but felt raw inside—and exhausted. A deep crevice split open inside me, warning me to prepare for long days of suffering, weeks and months of watching and waiting. Life had just become a thousand times more difficult. The prayers for healing were the first of many that still lay ahead.

I could only begin to grasp what life would be like without the laughter Mel's stories prompted. In the brief weeks since we'd met, I'd come to depend on his friendship, which was always extended to me with no requisite response or duty attached. I'd begun to dream of a future we would share on the homeplace. Now, instead, I faced possibly months of questions and loneliness and waiting.

It was sometime after Mel had been moved to Cleveland—a week or two perhaps—and started down the "long road" the doctor had described. I had spent hours beside him, but managed to continue working as best I could. Barbara had graciously given me a couple of days off each week.

Finally, one day I had gone out to Stony Ridge State Park by myself. I'd brought Buster home with me and he trailed along, bouncing into the brush, hoping to scare out rabbits that were hard to find that time of year. As I walked on the now-deserted paths, kicking dry leaves with my hiking boots, my fists jammed into my squall jacket for warmth, I remembered something Mel had said. Maybe that was what first gave me hope and courage to face the uncertainties ahead.

I sat to rest on a rotting stump of a large oak that had been harvested years earlier. I contemplated the pile of stones clustered in front of me—not likely a natural phenomenon, but perhaps a cairn, a way marker to guide those passing through. As I sat in the cold on the old stump in the still air of winter, snow began drifting down. A gentle, kind, early season snow. It was a fresh breath of nature, which promised in an hour or two to cover everything over with the gentle goodness of a new day, a new time, a new life.

I sat there taking it all in and heard Mel's voice. I thought I'd forgotten it, the way you forget the things you haven't heard for a long time. The way you fear your mind will no longer remember the sight of a beloved face when it is gone. But the memory of his words and the sound of his voice came to me through the snowfall. Yes, our memories do hold sound and sight. I imagined I heard him speak. I imagined not only his voice, but I heard his message: "I don't know, Angie . . . I don't know. All I know is that when we live passionately and enter into the spirit of the Creator, we can touch the holy in ourselves and others. . . . Maybe our journey really begins in these moments of grace and opportunity—these times when life looks most empty and bleak."

I sat a long time with this truth and then rose and wandered back to my car, back to my empty house, where I sat wishing for the phone to ring. Wishing for the sound of his voice. Feeling needy and wishing for some small comfort. But grateful I had known love, whatever tomorrow had in store for us.

"Maybe," I whispered to Mel, "maybe you are right, but I'm still not sure."

22

I HAD COME TO THE FARM to be with Mel. With the spirit of Mel. Christmas and all the holiday festivities were over, thankfully, and it was a weekend of rest and retreat. Until then, most of my free time had been spent in Cleveland at the hospital. But the day before, as I stood by Mel's bedside, when I reached for his hand to hold it as I'd been doing for weeks, he squeezed my hand. He didn't speak, but his eyes were open. He was looking around the room and then he saw me. I wondered if he knew me.

"Mel. Hi. Do you know where you are? Do you know who I am?"

And then came that longed-for response. Just a squeeze of the hand. Only that. But I knew it meant there was a future waiting for us.

I called Rhonda and told her the good news. "You need a retreat, Angie," she told me. "Take a day off from the hospital now and rest. Get away a little. You're going to burn out if you're not careful."

I knew she was right. And there was no question in my mind where I would retreat to: my homeplace.

When I arrived, I made a fire in the stove in Mel's front room. I'd carried enough firewood into the house to fill the wood box beside the stove, enough for the whole weekend. And as I carried the wood Mel had cut and stacked before that fateful Thanksgiving, I thought about how suffering is a weight you carry with you. It's a temporary burden, like that wood, but more difficult when you don't know how long it will last or where the present circumstance will end up. I wished I could lay suffering and questions about the future aside and move on. I'd suffered before, I knew, but no matter how much, it had never been like what I was experiencing now.

In Mel's place, as the embers glowed and the warmth spread, I sat in his front room and prayed my prayers, which had so many fewer words than the Mennonites'. I'd come to think that just a breath in and out can be a prayer for me. Sometimes I hadn't the strength for more. And like the Quaker I once was, I'd also come to believe that sitting in silence and listening can do as much for the world and for me as words can.

Sitting there, I replayed everything that had happened between Mel and me. I recognized each moment as *kairos*. Moments, so many moments of grace stretched between us. Rhonda has assured me that "moments of grace and opportunity" are as plentiful as the God who scatters them over our days. I'd had to believe her about that, because I couldn't see the truth of it then, in my dark night of the soul.

℃

All during January—the coldest days—I continued to go to the hospital. And I walked. Sometimes after I came home late at night I'd just start out walking, trying to walk away from the terrible loneliness and emptiness. Crying and praying and holding on to all that has been ripped from my life.

Then one Saturday morning, very early in the new year, I was awakened by—who knows what? It was four a.m., and it was dark and cold. In the latest wave of sadness, I dressed in my down parka, a wool scarf, mittens, and fleece-lined boots. The heavy snow we'd had a week earlier had melted and then frozen again, so there were trenches wherever wheels had gone the day before. Under my boots, the frozen snow cracked and crunched. Inside my mitten, I carried a wad of tissues, for I knew I would need them.

On into the dark I walked, and the momentum of my footsteps seemed to march me somehow away from the dark grief of the coldest, and perhaps also the longest, night of the winter.

As I walked it seemed as if the conversations, the stories, and the walks with Mel had happened years ago, not just two months ago. Things had changed so much in such a short time. In some ways, there was little in this present life that even resembled that other time. I knew deep within this wasn't really true. I knew there would come a time when I would be able to put together that other life with the present one. But not yet.

"You have everything you need." I seemed to hear a whisper in my heart telling me something I knew but still failed to trust.

Sweet moments—*kairos*. I recalled them one by one: that first evening when I entered Mel's dark kitchen and sat with him and Darwin; Mel and I getting to know one another over dinners and during conversations and in brief moments together; Mel's horses and our beautiful ride up to the ridge and down into God's Hollow. I remembered too Mel's passion for all the things that mattered most: his love of the land, his care for others, his friendly, kind-hearted welcome of everyone on the Thanksgiving weekend at his home; his determination to do something to improve the world, even for the children of far-off Laos.

And I revisited the fateful weekend that led to what we faced. Out on the farm my prayers had finally become true communion with God. I was no longer begging and pleading, but entering into God's presence. It was as if being at the homeplace, when Mel was absent, had taught me the lesson of finding the Spirit of the Creator. Sometimes on the long drive home from University Hospital in Cleveland I cried and pleaded with God to let Mel live, to let him recover. But this time, I felt a sense of surrender.

I'd been getting to know Mel's family. There were plenty of them too, all willing to take turns staying with him. They gave me a place among them, although we had just met on that Thanksgiving Day. But after the accident, we sat beside our loved one, not sure if he heard us or if he would ever awaken to know our names or see our faces. We all knew he would have to learn to walk again, and we knew that farm work would be out of the question for months. Yet that still seemed a long way off. "Perhaps during spring he will be in rehab," we said as we wiped the tears that kept gathering every time we thought of Mel and the suffering that still lay ahead.

As I trudged the dark road that winter morning, I thought about the day I'd gotten lost, and about finding my way to the homeplace. The journey itself was one story. But I remembered, too, all the other stories shared along the way. My world had changed because I'd found someone who really cared. Not just *one* person really, but a community I had discovered or in some ways even helped to create.

I was concerned about Darwin. He was struggling beyond belief. He sat at the hospital day after day, wrapped in a Mexican blanket someone had brought him. He was attending to Mel as if he could somehow make it up to him—the injury, the accident. Who can know if Mel had any idea that Darwin was the cause? Would Mel forgive him? Would any of us? I hoped Mel could hear Darwin talking to him and would know how sorry he was.

But at least I knew he'd heard me.

Darwin and me, we had both been telling him we loved him and wanted him to come back to life so he could share it with us, no matter what that might mean. Rhonda had talked about all of this with us, of course. What a blessing to know that our burdens could be shared among friends.

"Be grateful," I heard Rhonda saying as I trudged through the icy winter. "Whenever you think about the journey, about the people you've met along the way, about the places you've been, the things you've seen, the things you've done, be grateful." She knew better than to urge me to paint. That would wait for next season.

And so I walked on in the dark.

That's how life is sometimes. It is a walk uphill in the dark. I suppose the words "Enjoy the journey" are a platitude, given my new perspective. But if you can't enjoy the journey, as Mel once advised, at least live it, even with all its questions.

When I finally trudged home, it was getting light. The headlights of the Jeep delivering the morning *Repositor* came into view just as the first tinge of light appeared in the sky. I shivered in the cold and thought with gratitude of all my friends.

I'd turned the corner out there on that frozen back road. When I got back to my warm house, I was ever so slightly closer to something intangible, something called hope.

Epilogue

"WHAT IS THIS PLACE, where we are meeting? Only a house, the earth its floor . . ." The words to Rhonda's favorite hymn come to me in late February. Mel will be coming home soon. Finally I think of this place as Mel's homeplace again. We will name it that—or rather, it is already named. Darwin and I had a sign made. It's our surprise for Mel's homecoming, because we do believe he's coming home. It's just a matter of time. We've already put our sign up at the end of the lane. It says "Mel's Homeplace," just the way everyone always calls this farm.

It hasn't changed here in the house, except for the fact the kitchen is neater than Mel would keep it. There's evidence Paulie's family, or maybe James and Dorothy, moved some things around. But for the most part, the boxes and crates are still where Mel left them Thanksgiving afternoon.

I take in my surroundings, the comfortable things I recognize, like that hand-crocheted afghan thrown over the sofa, the old lamp with its yellowed shade and tarnished base, the antique cross-stitch sampler that reminds "To err is human, to forgive, divine." My eye rests on the huge, stainless-steel teakettle on the back burner of the stove, and I smile remembering Mel's story about the cookware salesman.

I am sitting once more in the perfect chair that holds me so tenderly in its arms. On the nearby ottoman is a stack of books and journals that seem as though they've been left there for me. I sift through them. They are Mel's messages, chosen for me to read today.

There are chocolates waiting with the books. Another serendipitous moment, as if Mel knew back in November that I'd be coming by today and would need this sweetness and refreshment. I pick out what looks to be a caramel—that would be his favorite—and savor the sweetness of this place, this moment, the memory of Darwin and me sharing caramels in my office. Even in his absence, Mel is present, blessing me. It's up to me to use my imagination, to keep love alive while we wwork and hope for recovery.

Mel is with me in the scent of this homeplace, which smells like nowhere I've ever lived. Its pungent mixture of manure, garlic, and fish sauce, mingled with wood smoke and a closed-up, musty farmhouse, is like no other. The heart has a mind, a mind that remembers, and no matter where I go or what happens after this, I will carry the goodness of my *kairos* journey with me. I feel the pleasure of his presence and imagine his eyes as they met mine when we walked together here on this farm and that day out on the trail.

Memory is all I have today. For now I need to find a way to substitute one thing for another. This I know. Love, I am thinking, is first of all comfort. Feeling safe and cared for and valued for who we are. This is what I try to offer my People, in my best case-manager moments, a way to find meaning and identity in their lives. And it starts with my recognition of their uniqueness. More often than I realize, in such simple and profound ways, my People help me too. They've comforted me in this tragedy and have given back what I've tried to offer.

But this afternoon at Mel's I know another comfort. I've found solace once again in the hills and fields and country roads, the geese flying overhead, the red-tail. Before I knew Mel, they called to me and I didn't notice them at all. Now they inhabit my world as companions, even messengers of hope for a better future.

And I've found comfort in my prayers, even when they are nothing but a sigh, some unexpressed truth held in my heart. I've learned to feel comforted every time I slow down. Every time I pet my cat or romp with Buster. In the spring, I'll see life renewed in the wildflowers, the clouds overhead, the farmers back in the fields plowing. Whether or not Mel will return as I once knew him, the comfort I've learned to receive through him will live on. All of this is Mel—his spirit.

I will be comforted with the beauty of nature that is everywhere, with memories of things said, conversations. And even the conversations we didn't have, because of their potential in some other time and place, or even perhaps with other people. I will be comforted by all these memories, rich and aromatic, like the first sip of the first cup of coffee of the day. These simple things are part of the life we once had together.

In my reminiscing this morning, Mel seems as close as ever. As I sit there in his chair, thinking of him, hope seems to sneak up on me, despite my fears and the bone-deep tiredness of waiting for something to change. I sit until I finally believe. We do have a future, as unknown as it still remains. My *kairos* journey started when I got lost and continues here.

Mel will come back to his homeplace someday—soon. We'll take each step together. He will help me. And I will help him. Maybe next week, perhaps in a month. It could be late spring.

I know now: Whenever Mel comes home, I'll be near-by to walk with him. But for these few moments I rest in his chair and set my eyes on the fields just beyond the door.

About
the
Author

Kairos is Joanne Lehman's first novel. In 2004, she won the Kent State University Wick Poetry Chapbook Competitions for her collection *Morning Song*. She was employed for ten years as a community relations specialist for the Mental Health and Recovery Board of Wayne and Holmes Counties, Ohio, and was editor of the *Ohio Evangel*, a Mennonite periodical. Her poetry and essays have appeared in *Artful Dodge, Farming Magazine, The Mennonite, DreamSeeker, Rejoice, Christian Living,* and local newspapers. She is the author of *Traces of Treasure: Quest for God in the Commonplace* (Herald Press, 1994). She lives in Apple Creek, Ohio, with her husband, Ralph. They have two children and four grandchildren.